She Hea

He'd be a fastidious o
name sounded tediou

Tyrus—tyrant, she thought. The car door slammed
and she made another attempt at spontaneous word
association. "Tyrannosaurus...?"

So the man was an old dinosaur. As long as he paid his
rent and kept to himself they could have an occasional
game of dominoes.

The door rattled under the force of a set of determined
knuckles, and Anny felt her preconceived ideas of
Tyrus Clay dissolve into something less reassuring.
"Mr. Clay?" she hazarded.

The man whose shoulders practically blocked her
doorway was a world apart from what she'd expected.
Scratch the dominoes, Anny mused. She'd sooner play
games with a shark.

Dear Reader:

SILHOUETTE DESIRE is an exciting new line of contemporary romances from Silhouette Books. During the past year, many Silhouette readers have written in telling us what other types of stories they'd like to read from Silhouette, and we've kept these comments and suggestions in mind in developing SILHOUETTE DESIRE.

DESIREs feature all of the elements you like to see in a romance, plus a more sensual, provocative story. So if you want to experience all the excitement, passion and joy of falling in love, then SILHOUETTE DESIRE is for you.

For more details write to:

Jane Nicholls
Silhouette Books
PO Box 236
Thornton Road
Croydon
Surrey CR9 3RU

DIXIE BROWNING
A Bird in Hand

Silhouette Desire

Originally Published by Silhouette Books
division of
Harlequin Enterprises Ltd.

All the characters in this book have no existence outside the
imagination of the Author, and have no relation whatsoever to
anyone bearing the same name or names. They are not even dis-
tantly inspired by any individual known or unknown to the Author,
and all the incidents are pure invention.

The text of this publication or any part thereof may not be repro-
duced or transmitted in any form or by any means, electronic or
mechanical, including photocopying, recording, storage in an
information retrieval system, or otherwise, without the written
permission of the publisher.

This book is sold subject to the condition that it shall not, by way
of trade or otherwise, be lent, resold, hired out or otherwise cir-
culated without the prior consent of the publisher in any form of
binding or cover other than that in which it is published and
without a similar condition including this condition being imposed
on the subsequent purchaser.

DIXIE BROWNING
is a native of North Carolina. When she isn't traveling to research her books, she divides her time between her home in Winston-Salem and her cottage at Buxton on Hatteras Island.

Other Silhouette Books by Dixie Browning

Silhouette Desire

Shadow of Yesterday
Image of Love
The Hawk and the Honey
Late Rising Moon
Stormwatch
The Tender Barbarian
Matchmaker's Moon

Silhouette Special Edition

Finders Keepers
Reach Out to Cherish
Just Deserts
Time and Tide
By Any Other Name

*For further information about
Silhouette Books please write to:*

Jane Nicholls
Silhouette Books
PO Box 236
Thornton Road
Croydon
Surrey CR9 3RU

One

Anny was on her knees stuffing magazines into the closet when she heard the car turn off the pavement onto the graveled road. "Beans! The old relic could at least have had the decency to wait until I was ready for him," she muttered into the neck of her baggy sweat shirt.

The untidy stack slithered across the closet floor again, and in desperation she shoved them back and blocked their escape with a mismatched pair of boots. A spider web trailed across her arm, and she eyed its displaced inhabitant sympathetically. "We're being invaded again, sport. Keep a low profile for the next three months and you can go on defending my household from flying insects, but set one foot in that bedroom I just cleaned and out you go."

Anny had a high tolerance for small creatures, a lesser one for the roomers she took in for a few months each year through the university housing program. After six years of living alone, she valued her privacy.

Unfortunately, her privacy had a leaky roof, and while her earnings as an illustrator for a small press supported her and her assorted interests quite nicely, that income, even with the additional free-lance jobs that came her way, didn't allow for the renovation of the one-hundred-eleven-year-old house she'd inherited.

She heard the car hit the pothole and turn into her driveway. "Oh, beans," she grumbled again, shutting the closet door and glancing about the living room in frustration. There was no time to change into anything more respectable, and she'd truly meant to dress up and play lady long enough to make a decent first impression. She desperately needed a shower, too. She'd just have to try to stay downwind of the old boy and hope his senses were failing with age.

Ordinarily, grooming was the least of her worries. The bonding period between landlady and tenant was a critical time, though, and Anny was at her most efficient when it came to saving herself work. She'd long since discovered that if she made the effort to appear fastidious for the first few days, her paying guests would respond in kind. As a result, instead of having a pigsty to cope with once a week, she could usually get by with a change of linens and a quick once-over.

The system worked. She'd tried it both ways, and while the initial effort was always a pain, it was definitely energy-efficient.

Over the years Anny had come to terms with her house. On rainy days she made a stab at doing what had to be done. On all other days she divided her time between the acres of woods that bordered the river, where she did field sketches, hunted for traces of buried history and bird-watched, and her studio, where she perfected her work until it was ready to turn over to the publisher.

In deference to the crisp October weather, the front door stood open. Anny dusted off her knees and brushed the webs from her wrist while she watched a low-slung car run the gamut of potholes and pull up before her front door.

Oh, Lord! Her hands were filthy, her hair was a haystack, and there was no time! She yanked off her scarf and finger-combed the flyaway strands. She'd come to think of her hair as camel-tan, but with all the dust and cobwebs, it was probably elephant-gray at the moment.

And he'd be a fastidious old worrywart. The very name sounded tedious: Tyrus Clay.

All she knew about him was that he'd retired recently. and was to spend three months at Duke University in an advisory capacity doing something or other at the F. P. Hall Laboratory. For the life of her she couldn't remember which department that was, but the name Tyrus Clay conjured up visions of a withered little man who'd spent a lifetime hunched over dusty clay tablets and brittle rolls of papyrus.

The man was a retired Egyptologist, Anny decided on the spot. She'd been practicing sudden revelations and flashes of insight ever since she'd started reading her way through the occult section of the library she'd inherited along with the house.

Another flash occurred. "Or a tyrant," she muttered aloud. *Tyrus—tyrant.* Just as the car door slammed, she made one more attempt at spontaneous word association. "Tyrannosaurus?"

All right, so the man was an old dinosaur. Whatever his disposition, he'd be on campus most of the time. As long as he paid his rent and didn't ask more of her than a weekly room cleaning and maybe an occasional game of dominoes, they'd get along. She had her own life to live, and she couldn't allow herself to grow attached to another lonely old man just because he was living under her roof.

The screened door rattled under the force of a set of determined knuckles, and Anny felt her preconceived ideas of Tyrus Clay dissolve into something slightly less reassuring. She tried for a cool smile of welcome. The smile faltered, struggled to rekindle, then died altogether. "Mr. Clay?" she hazarded. "Mr. Tyrus Clay? *Senior?*" she added for good measure.

"Tyrus Clay. Is this the Cousins residence? Go find Mrs. Cousins for me, will you?"

The man whose shoulders practically blocked her wide front door was a world apart from what she'd expected. Scratch the dominoes, Anny mused. She'd sooner play games with a shark.

"Did you have any trouble finding the place?" she asked when she'd recovered most of her composure. "I offered to do a map, but the woman at the housing office said it might put people off—if they thought they needed a map, I mean...to get here, that is." Her voice trailed off as she experienced a rush of feeling that left her uncomfortably warm.

In a level baritone that revealed nothing at all of his background, Tyrus Clay said, "No problems. It's farther than I expected."

The warmth fled, leaving her shaken. *It's too far,* she interpreted, despair all tangled up with the confusing feelings that churned through her. "Well, at least it's restful out here in the country. And once you know the shortcuts, it doesn't take all that long to get to town." *He's not going to stay.* She felt a stab of disappointment that had nothing to do with her roofing fund. "Still," she said, managing a smile, "I suppose one man's 'restful' is another man's 'buried alive.' Do you want to come in and look around, anyway, as long as you're here?"

Anny had always prided herself on being the most pragmatic of woman. Now she suddenly felt like crying, and all because this stranger who stood blocking her doorway didn't seem to care for her house or its location.

It must be a phase of the moon, she rationalized. She'd wept over some silly things in her life, but this was a new low.

The shoulders moved away from the doorway, accompanied by the rest of a body that could have belonged to a decathlon athlete. Anny got her first really good look at his face. In spite of lines that might have been etched by ill temper, dissipation, or a combination of both, Tyrus Clay possessed the most arrogantly handsome face she'd ever seen in her long and uneventful life.

"I'm Anny Lee Cousins. This is my house, Mr. Clay." She extended her hand. Catching sight of her grimy nails, she swiftly withdrew it. "You're not at all what I expected, you know," she added with characteristic candor.

Her remark was met with a flinty look that spoke volumes. All right, so she wasn't his idea of a model landlady, either. She'd been caught at a disadvantage. Appearances had become less and less important to her over the years, but for the first time she wished she hadn't made quite such an obsession of denying her background.

Tyrus's teeth gritted tightly as he contained his irritation. Dammit! He should have thought to ask. He'd specified something quiet and solitary, but he hadn't given a thought beyond that. She was certainly not much to look at, but she was decidedly female. The last thing he needed now was a constant reminder of a condition he'd be better off forgetting—at least until he could do something about it.

If he weren't so damned bushed he'd get back in the car, head for the coast, and forget the whole thing. He must have been out of his head to think he could just pull up stakes, move inland, and step into an academic situation with no problem.

The silence grew painfully thin, and Anny hurried to fill it. "I suppose you were expecting something a little more...uh..." She shrugged, never taking her eyes from the lean, worn face. The initial effect was beginning to fade now, but there was no escaping the fact that the man packed a wallop! "The house was built in the late 1800s. That's not really old by Hillsborough standards, but if you're a history buff..."

Scornful silence met her suggestion, and Anny twisted her hands together. Did he *look* like a history buff?

He looked like a soldier of fortune, she acknowledged with a return of that uncomfortable warmth. He looked like a buccaneer. He looked like the epitome of every woman's secret fantasy—strong, beautiful, radiating virility—even though at the moment he was obviously tired and out of sorts. "It sits on fifteen acres," she continued, "and there's nothing around for miles except the river and the woods." Helplessly, she allowed her gaze to linger on the complex curves of his mouth. "Naturally, if you don't think you'll be happy here, I won't hold you to the agreement, Mr. Clay. I realize that this sort of place isn't to everyone's taste."

"I signed an agreement at the housing office for three months, but if you want to back out, Mrs. Cousins, I'll find something else. I can go to a hotel, or even live on campus for the few months I'll be here."

She could sense his withdrawal and it struck sparks off her pride. If the agreement was going to be broken, she preferred to do the breaking. For once she'd like to be the rejector instead of the rejectee. "If you don't feel you'd be comfortable here, Mr. Clay, I certainly wouldn't want you to stay." Perhaps that would be best all around, she concluded reluctantly. Better for her, at any rate. Tyrus Clay was hardly the sort of man a woman could ignore, and at this point in her life, she didn't need trouble of *that* sort.

Across the comfortably shabby room, with a low autumn sun highlighting the irregularities in the heart-pine floor between them, Ty braced his feet at the ready. The signal would have been recognized in any waterfront bar in the world. "Don't put words in my mouth. On second thought, I believe I'm going to have to hold you to the agreement, Mrs. Cousins. I'm in no mood to start looking for another place at this late date."

"It's Miss—*Miss* Cousins," Anny corrected, dismayed at the degree of relief that flowed through her. "But if you think you might be staying here, I suppose you may as well call me Anny."

"Miss Cousins, I just finished telling you that I *will* be staying here. And just so we both know where we stand, my requirements are few and simple. During the short time I'm here, I'll appreciate quietness, an absence of companionship, and the privilege of being discourteous whenever the mood strikes me.'' His eyes held all the warmth of surgical steel. ''I tell you this in case you harbor any ideas to the contrary. I am *not* a happy man, Miss Cousins. I am not a *genial* man. If your skin is as thin as it looks under all that grime, I'd advise you to ignore me completely and go about your business as though I weren't even in the house. I believe there was some mention of a separate outside staircase so that I can come and go without having to go through your living quarters?''

As Anny digested the words spoken with such a deadly lack of emphasis, the planes of her rather unremarkable face underwent a subtle change. Her shell once more securely in place, she said, ''It sounds as if we both want the same thing, Mr. Clay. I assure you, companionship is the last thing on my mind. Now that we understand each other, if you'd care to bring in your bags, I'll show you to your room.''

She refused to allow his rudeness to get under her skin. Did it ever occur to him that her own privacy was every bit as valuable to her as his was to him? ''You're free to use the kitchen for breakfast. The upstairs bath is all yours. I use the other room up there as a studio, but if the sound of a crow-quill pen scratching on illustration board bothers you, I'll make other arrangements.''

''Show me around first. I'll bring my bags up later.'' Grimly, Tyrus followed her up a set of narrow, sloping stairs that would have been condemned outright in any public building. If she'd told him to come along and see his quarters first and collect his bags later, he'd have done just the opposite.

His bleak gaze moved over the trim backside in the clinging pants as it swayed up the stairs ahead of him.

Dammit! It had reached the point of being ludicrous, the way he had to keep on proving something to himself. Let him come within range of any passable woman and he immediately started throwing his weight around.

And this one was barely passable: the face of a hungry kid, all eyes and cheekbones, and the grooming habits of a bag lady.

Still, it was better than living in an apartment in town—or, still worse, on campus, where he'd be subjected to the sight of all those nubile coeds in their painted-on jeans. He'd specified something quiet and isolated, and this place seemed to fill the bill on that score, at least. If his complete recovery depended on exercise, diet, and relaxation, then this was as good a place as any to get on with it.

Anny was on her best behavior for the better part of a week. She arose at six, made her breakfast, which might consist of raw oatmeal and wheat germ with chopped apple, or cold pizza and chocolate ice cream, depending on the mood of the moment and the contents of the refrigerator. She waited until Tyrus had driven into Durham each day before going up to her studio, where she worked until early afternoon. Then, armed with camera, sketch pads, binoculars, and a metal detector, she headed for the woods to work and play until starvation drove her home again.

By that time, her tenant's car was usually parked in the designated place under the red oak tree. She neither saw nor heard the man. Whatever he found to occupy his free time, he was quiet about it. She might as well have been alone in the house.

Not that it bothered her. Her initial reaction to Tyrus had been decidedly out of character; she'd put it down to a seasonal hormonal imbalance or a phase of the moon, something that could be explained away by perfectly rational factors. She was *not* the fluttery type.

Anny enjoyed her solitary life-style. Now and then she drove to Charlotte and spent a weekend with Susan Macklin, friend and editor-in-chief of Persimmon Press. She still dated now and then, and her parents always stopped off on their seasonal migrations, but Anny considered herself a loner at heart. She'd established a satisfying life for herself, first with Hannibal, and then, after he'd died, alone. It suited her.

Normally, she'd have gone upstairs two or three nights a week and worked far into the morning hours, but she'd found it impossible to concentrate with Tyrus in the next room, and she'd given up trying. Odd, the effect he had on her. Anny had long since passed beyond the impressionable stage where men were concerned.

Her last two paying guests had been women, a situation not without its own drawbacks. They'd been far more fastidious than the men, which had been both good and bad. While they'd kept their own rooms in perfect order, they'd both had an aversion to finding frozen mice thawing on a sunny windowsill. She'd explained about her babies and offered them a quick peek, but it hadn't helped. Granted, baby owls weren't at their most attractive at that early stage of development, particularly with their greedy little beaks all caked with pigeon bisque. Still, they were babies. She'd have thought the maternal instinct would overcome a few qualms.

At least with Tyrus Clay she wouldn't have to juggle feeding schedules and guest privileges. This time of year, any birds she got would be injured adults that would be taken immediately to the mews. If she could remember to thaw the mice in her own room instead of tossing the plastic bag onto the nearest sunny windowsill, she should be safe enough.

Unwilling to risk a confrontation, Anny worked in the studio mornings after Tyrus left for Durham. At night, she continued her self-imposed task of reading her way through the shelves of books she'd inherited, skimming some, passing up those written in Latin altogether, and devouring others. Her late Great-uncle Hannibal, from whom she'd inherited the house and its contents, had had surprisingly catholic tastes in literature.

Her concentration was suffering badly. All week she'd felt the presence of Tyrus Clay looming over her like a thundercloud. While he kept to his room upstairs, Anny remained downstairs, reading and making minor revisions to the day's field drawings. Now and then she glanced up. He was so quiet up there. Either he read even more than she did, or he came home after dinner each night and went straight to bed. Didn't the man know how unhealthy it was to eat a large dinner and go right to sleep?

At least he was neat. In fact, his precision bed-making, the orderliness of his books and the few items of clothing she'd glimpsed through the closet door were enough to put her own haphazard housekeeping to shame.

As the second week ended, Anny congratulated herself. So far, without coming to blows, they'd exchanged exactly five good-mornings and three good-afternoons. Plus, she added with her usual candor, a thorough survey of respective topographies.

Unfortunately, what she'd seen had only strengthened her first impression: here was a hunk of the first magnitude. Well over six feet, he was in excellent physical condition in spite of a look of tension that manifested itself in a perennial scowl and a terse quality of speech that stopped just short of actual rudeness. His face was deeply tanned, and his body revealed none of the slackness usually associated with the sedentary habits of an academic profession. "Leather stretched over steel" was the way she characterized him to herself.

Under a well-defined brow, his eyes were the color of a particularly lovely shade of flint she'd found recently—more blue than gray. His hair, so black as to defy the light, was laced with random silver threads. At odd moments she found herself wondering if that deeply carved upper lip and the fuller, if equally firm, lower one could express any emotion other than impatience.

In fact, she found herself thinking entirely too much about his lips.

Not that he hadn't scrutinized her with equal thoroughness, Anny recalled with a flurry of subliminal excitement. All morning long as she sketched the rock formations and the variety of vegetation that clung to the banks of the Eno River, she was bothered by the memory of those intense, flintlike eyes as they'd moved over her body outside the kitchen door this morning. As always, her face was without makeup, nor could her costume be called seductive. She was wearing an ancient pair of corduroy jeans and a ribbed cotton pullover that had grown shapeless through years of careless washing, neither of which had been proof against Tyrus's frank appraisal.

What had he thought of her?

More to the point, why was she even wondering about something so silly? It had been ages since she'd cared what any man thought of her. As a matter of pure survival, Anny had learned to base her self-value on something more important than other people's opinions.

Words she'd overheard her father say at her fifteenth birthday party drifted back to her, and Anny's chin lifted imperceptibly.

"Claire, the child defeats me. She's so sullen all the time. Were you such a mess at fifteen? Is it a phase girls go through? If it weren't for the fact that the poor girl's got my mother's cheekbones and your father's stubbornness, I'd swear she was no spawn of ours. I can't deal with her." He'd gestured helplessly with narrow, flawlessly manicured hands, as Anny, miserable in an expensive dress that was snug in all the wrong places, had gazed through the door. "I can't even *dress* her properly. She's such a—"

"Evan, lower your voice! At least Annabelle's a nice child. Her eyes are really lovely, and in ten years or so she'll grow to the cheekbones." Claire's drawl had softened so that Anny had had to strain to hear. "I suppose I could take her to Phoenix in January, but then what would I do with her? After the spa, I'm going ahead to Palm Springs with Minnie, and I certainly don't want—" The flick of a lighter and a deep sigh had covered the rest of the words. Anny hadn't needed to hear them. "Meanwhile, if you could prevail on Zivia not to make *ponchki* more than once a month, the poor child might start to shed some of that baby fat."

Evan Cousins, a slight, dark man with a narrow, clever face, was a designer of women's clothing with a small string of boutiques scattered among some half dozen resorts. As Ivan Koscienski, he'd come from New Jersey to North Carolina to study textile engineering. In his second year he'd met Claire LeMontrose of the Orange County LeMontroses, and they'd fallen in love almost immediately. Claire had been only too glad for a chance to escape a dull existence circumscribed by too much family pride and too little money.

They'd eloped shortly after Evan had petitioned the courts to have his name changed from Ivan Koscienski to Evan Cousins. He'd have taken the LeMontrose name if Claire's father hadn't threatened his life.

Anny loved her parents in a detached sort of way, even though she sometimes felt as if they weren't quite real. It wasn't their fault that as an only child in a world of sophisticated adults, she'd always felt miserably out of place.

After years of moving with the season from Bar Harbor to Hilton Head to Palm Springs, with boarding schools and summer camps taking up the slack, she'd finally rebelled. Enrolling in the University of North Carolina, she'd immersed herself in books. The summer after her first year, she'd gone to her father's old home in New Jersey in search of family, finding only a distant cousin. They'd disliked each other on sight.

On the maternal side, she'd found Great-uncle Hannibal LeMontrose. Prepared for a cool reception, she'd found herself drawn into his gentle world almost without realizing it.

Gradually, Anny had discovered in herself a strong set of values, of priorities that were radically different from those of her parents. Her own personality had begun to emerge.

Spending her vacations with Hannibal in the old house that had settled over the years until there wasn't a square corner or a level surface in it had accelerated the process. Anny had moved in with him after graduation. In the few years before he died, she'd found something of lasting value in the companionship of the gentle, eccentric old man who read Latin for pleasure and kept bees for profit. She also found something in the red earth of North Carolina that she'd never found in the more exotic turf of any exclusive resort—a sense of belonging.

Now, eyeing the dark-centered thunderheads that clambered over the treetops, Anny began gathering up her scattered gear. Had she or had she not remembered to empty the buckets in the attic after the last deluge? Her efficiency, spotty at best, had suffered from a slight distraction lately.

Still, the weather had been unseasonally warm until recently. Even if she'd forgotten, evaporation had probably done the trick. The rain was bad enough; overflowing buckets she could do without.

A red-tailed hawk soared overhead, and Anny stopped to watch, her sympathies divided between the graceful predator and its small, unwary prey. Licensed by the state wildlife commission to rehabilitate raptors, she'd learned to love them both.

And that, she recalled ruefully as she stuffed her drawing pens under the flap of her knapsack and slipped a protective plastic bag over the head of her detector, was just one more thing her parents couldn't understand. A parakeet or a cockatiel, fine—but owls? Hideous little creatures that devoured disgusting things in her kitchen?

"Darling, if only you weren't so...earthy." Her father's despairing words came back to her, and she grinned. Ever hopeful, he'd dropped in for a quick visit on his way to New York a few months before, bringing with him the unmarried manager of one of his boutiques.

Evan had tried to call from the airport, but she'd taken the phone off the hook in order to work undisturbed. They'd rented a car, and Anny had been caught in her usual state of disarray as she doled eyedropper servings of high-protein-blenderized pigeon. There'd been no way she could stop, not until all the greedy little bellies were satisfied, nor had they cared to join her, which was just as well. She tried hard to keep her hatchlings from being imprinted, as their later survival depended on their fear of the human species.

She'd finished her task, all the while imagining Evan's impressions of her housekeeping standards and her life-style. He'd given up offering to find her a maid and was now determined to find her a husband, someone to take her away from it all.

From the living room she'd heard a grunt of disapproval; he'd spotted the stacks of books on the floor beside the couch, the row of shoes under the coffee table, or the milkweed pods that had shed all over the rug.

Poor Evan. The simplicity of her tastes continued to elude him. He considered her mad to bury herself in the backwoods. He'd been delighted when she'd decided to study art, furious when she'd refused to join his design department, and he'd done his best to lure her back to civilization, using as bait the younger of his more eligible acquaintances.

A spatter of rain struck her, and Anny began to jog. Earthy, he'd called her. Earthy wasn't so bad. She'd been called worse things: stubborn, prudish, lazy, out of touch with reality. Earthy was just fine, as long as one didn't expect impossible and unrealistic things. And Anny didn't.

The rain began coming down in earnest, and she ducked her head and ran, feeling the slap of wet cotton knit against her bare skin. She'd forgotten to bring a jacket.

Had she remembered to mention the leaks in his room to Tyrus? Probably not. Still, what could he do? Move out? She almost wished he would. Lately, she'd been finding it almost impossible to relax, just knowing he was up there.

Two

Tyrus lay on the bed, one arm flung across his eyes as he attempted to focus his mind on the knotted muscles at the back of his neck. He swore softly; it wasn't going to work. Neither the setup on campus nor this quasi-mystical exercise that was supposed to bring peace, tranquility, and, more importantly, the return of his ability to function as a man. The more times he went through this damned, idiotic drill, ordering each separate part of his body to let go, the more he felt like a complete fool, and that in turn wiped out any possible benefits he might otherwise have gained.

Big toe, relax, he willed grimly. *Plantar arch, relax!*

Starting with the feet, he could make it just about as far up as the muscles of his thighs. Alternatively, he could begin with his scalp and work down to his abdominal muscles. But the minute he tried to exert his will on the most vital area of a man's anatomy, his mind tuned in an instant replay of that last scene with Cass, and his head started throbbing, the pulse just under his jaw started hammering, and he could actually feel the tension in his body begin to rise.

All except where it counted.

Opening his eyes, Ty scowled up at the ceiling. What the hell was going on up there—an invasion of mice? Squirrels hauling in a winter's supply of nuts? He swore in disgust; when he blew it, he really blew it all the way. Permanently beached, physically *hors de combat*, and he'd topped it off by agreeing to move into a leaking old ruin with a landlady who was…well, strange, at the very least.

If he'd needed any further inducement to go vegetarian, it had been the sight of that freezer compartment full of rodents, all neatly packaged in individual plastic bags. Since then, he'd got by on coffee and one big meal in the middle of the day, choosing from what was available and allowable. If starving his body of all decent food was going to help him get back on track again, he'd do it. He'd do it if it killed him. Only the regime also called for exercise. Where was the energy supposed to come from? Carrots? Cucumbers? He was supposed to exercise like a horse and eat like a rabbit?

Ty could already feel a certain ominous slackness invading his muscles, and with the hypochondriac reaction of a man who'd never been sick a day in his life, he reached for his pulse and fought back a fresh attack of self-pity.

The medic's raspy drawl came back to him: "Exercise and diet, son, there's your salvation. Follow the diet sheets I've given you and get plenty of exercise and relaxation. Check back in about three weeks and we'll see how it's going."

Exercise. What the devil was he expected to do, take up golf? Trade in his diving gear for a leotard and join a bunch of panting, sweating bodies in one of those aerobic dance classes? Of the two forms of exercise he knew best, one had been forbidden and the other had been rendered impossible.

From overhead came the odd scrabbling noise again. A trickle of fine dust sifted down on his face, and he sneezed. God, what next? It wasn't bad enough that he was stuck in a windowless office all day with nothing to do but shuffle papers, but did he also have to come home to *this*?

"I give up," he snarled aloud, rising from the rumpled bed with the lithe movement of a man in perfect control of every muscle in his body.

Only he wasn't. After nearly thirty-eight years of perfect health, he'd been sidelined by hypertension, something he'd never even thought about.

It wasn't as though he'd expected to stay in the game forever. He'd been planning to retire from active diving in a few more years, anyhow. Shorty had already agreed to buy out his interest, with no stipulation as to how and when. With a run of good luck, they'd be square within six months, and Ty had thought he might buy himself a small fishing boat, something in the forty-five-to-fifty-foot range, and maybe a little place near the coast.

On the other hand, if the generator on the diveboat couldn't be rebuilt and Shorty had to replace that as well as the compressor, it could take awhile to settle things out. That was all right, too. He'd make out. He always had. He'd gone into partnership with Shorty Mc-

Pherson on no more than a handshake, and they'd parted on the same basis. In a field as risky as salvage diving, you didn't work with a man you couldn't trust.

The thing was, he wasn't ready to get out yet, dammit! He'd been diving all his life; it was all he knew. Once he'd gotten over the initial shock of being beached, he'd contacted the Duke Marine Labs at Beaufort with some notion of trading his twenty-odd years' experience at every type of diving under every sort of condition for a spot on the team.

For years he'd known about the work they were doing at the Marine Labs at Beaufort. He'd known less about the experimental work being done on the Durham campus with the simulated dive-tank program.

The call had paid off, if not quite the way he'd planned. He'd taken for granted that if he did decide to team up with the university's program, he'd be working at the coastal campus, close enough to Cass to try to persuade her to give him another chance.

Instead, he'd found himself agreeing to three months on the main campus at Durham before he even got a shot at anything else. They'd been reluctant to promise much, under the circumstances. Whether or not he ever took on more than a support role in the simulated experimental dive program would depend on his ability to pull his blood pressure back down to normal levels and maintain it. He'd had to talk incredibly fast to get that much of a concession.

Working in his favor were his years of deep-sea experience under varying conditions, attesting to the fact that he wasn't subject to high pressure nervous syndrome, which was the focus of the present series of studies. Ironically, it was the diving bell accident that had clinched it for him, the same accident that had started him thinking about getting out before the bone necrosis started, before his lungs and his ears went.

Commercial diving was a young man's game. At thirty-eight, Tyrus had lasted a lot longer than most. He'd planned to log a few more years on the oil rigs before heading for friendlier waters. The money was tops—the higher the risk, the higher the pay—but money wasn't everything. He'd learned that the hard way, and it had taken a hell of a lot out of him. He'd made himself go on diving after the accident, and that had weighed heavily in his favor.

He'd once heard someone trying to describe a diving bell as a hollow steel ball full of men, dangling on a chain and a rubber band under the surface of the water. Not a bad analogy, although the umbilical was a bit more important than a rubber band, and there was also a shackle that attached the chain to the ball. In diving, no small part was unimportant. A man's life could depend on something as trivial as a lousy ten-buck shackle.

They'd been hooka diving at four hundred fifty feet when the shackle had snapped. The bell had dropped another fifty feet on the slack in the umbilical before the deck crew had jammed the winch, stopping the fall of the bell. His buddy on that bounce had been a new kid, a skinny, brash young Texan whose career plan was to get in, grab the money, and get out. Working together, they'd been inspecting the damage after three weeks of unrelenting gale-force winds. The winds had finally slowed, but the seas were still running high, and there'd been a fierce current.

"What the hell happened?" Texas had screamed.

"Get the brakes on! Get the son-of-a-bitching brakes on!" Ty had yelled to the deck crew.

Communications had held, thank God. At that point they hadn't known that they were dangling at five hundred feet by the umbilical. Through the static, he could hear someone screaming something about a dead haul. Everyone on deck was talking at once, the bell was clanging against the rigging, and Texas was all but catatonic.

It had taken less than an hour to determine the extent of the problem. It had seemed like years. The shackle had broken, and before the umbilical winch could take up the slack, the bell had dropped, bouncing heavily. Pushed by the current, it had managed to get snagged in the rigging.

The umbilical was literally a lifeline. They were totally dependent on it for the mixture of gases they breathed, for the heat that kept them from freezing to death in the icy waters, for all communication with the rig. As big around as a man's biceps, it was made up of a number of components, each one of vital importance. If a single portion had snapped in the fall, if it had been damaged in any way, the results could have been disastrous.

And even if it held, the weather was a constant threat. They'd have to bring in a special repair team by helicopter, and no sane man would attempt a repair dive in seas over sixty feet. If the weather clamped down, they'd bought it; they'd both been coldly aware of the odds against them. The umbilical might hold the bell in suspension under normal conditions, but even under the best conditions, it would never support the tremendous weight in a haul. And they'd been tangled in the rigging with a damaged umbilical.

Luck had been with them that time, but Ty had come as close to the edge of hell as he cared to venture in this life. He'd hung on during the endless hours, holding the kid like a baby most of the time, hearing an incoherent confession, comforting with words that had come from a source he'd never questioned.

By the time they got to Aberdeen for the safety hearings, the cold sweats had ceased, and he'd practically stopped shaking. The kid had stuck with it, bouncing back with a resilience Ty could only envy, but as soon afterward as he could manage it, Ty had headed for the States. Once ashore, he'd tried to wipe out the whole episode by going on a monumental binge. It hadn't helped. It had been months before he could close the door on a room smaller than twelve by twelve, still longer before the nightmares had stopped.

He'd beat around the balmy islands of the Caribbean for a while and then moved on to the Gulf Coast, where he'd met Shorty McPherson. Chugging beers and chewing the stub of a dead cigar, Shorty had been trying to talk himself into going in hock for some much-needed new equipment. After due consideration—a matter of some half dozen beers—Tyrus had agreed to put up the money in trade for a share of the business.

He'd been thirty-five then. There'd been no hint of anything that would land him on shore behind a desk before he was forty. He'd figured he had at least ten more good years in which to taper off if he bypassed the deep stuff.

And then out of the blue, he'd lost everything. He'd managed to rationalize the slight dizziness he'd experienced once or twice by blaming his regulator. The headaches had been something else. It had been the headaches that had made him look up the nearest medic. Within a block of the waterfront, he'd found an M.D. who looked as though he'd had enough experience to know what he was talking about. With no attempt at a bedside manner, the man had laid it on the line.

"Son, your hell raising days are over," the old man had said flatly, stripping the cuff from Ty's arm. "Go on the way you've been going and you won't see forty. Your lungs are still sound, but your blood pressure's way into the red. Take my advice: get as far away from temptation as you can and learn a new trade. Otherwise, you'll try just one more dive, and then just one more, and one of 'em will be your last. Follow these instructions I'm going to give you and you stand a good chance of drawing your social security."

Stunned, Ty had told the man what he could do with his instructions and walked out.

The next morning he'd dived on a sunken trawler, and in no more than thirty feet of water, he'd had another one of those spells of disorientation. It had scared the hell out of him. He'd been on his back at the time, and again he'd tried to blame it on a faulty regulator, but he'd known better. His gear was in first-class condition. He wasn't.

If he'd still harbored any illusions about beating the odds, that had wiped them out. He'd had some close calls even before the bell accident, and any statistician knew that the odds worsened with every dive. Hell, he'd been at it for more than twenty years. He'd started out officially as a U.D.T. in Nam, but even before that, he'd been diving uncertified around Mexico. After Nam, he'd put in time with a marine repairs place in Galveston, done some salvage work out of Mobile, and then gone with the oil rigs, starting in the Gulf of Mexico and ending up in the North Sea.

For as long as he could remember, he'd put in six- and seven-day weeks diving on anything that might bring in a buck. And since he'd become part owner of a barge, a tug, and a mess of rusting machinery, he'd worked his tail off helping to maintain gear and equipment when he wasn't actually diving.

"Not married, are you?" the medic had asked when he'd gone back a week later.

Ty had thought of his long-term, open-ended relationship with Cass Valenti. "No."

"Hmm. Now, this drug I'm prescribing has been known to have a slight side effect on some men. Not all of 'em, though. If you were a married man, I'd want to talk things over with your wife. An understanding woman can make things a lot easier, if you know what I mean."

"Yeah, well, if I decide to take a wife, I'll make sure she's the understanding type, okay. Now, is that all? Sure you wouldn't like to try a few leeches?" The atmosphere was stifling him. He had to get out of there before his head rocked right off his body.

It had taken little more than a week to get his affairs in order. One thing he'd known instinctively; he couldn't stay on with Shorty and the crew and remain topside. One of these days he might be able to pull it off, but he didn't care to risk it now. The first time one of the other divers showed up with a head cold or a hangover, he'd be suiting up and going down.

He'd stashed away a little something in investments even before he'd thrown in with Shorty. The dividends wouldn't go far, and the Duke thing was little more than an interim measure, at best. He was too short on academics for anything permanent, even if he'd wanted it.

So...his diving days were over, and what did he have to show for it? As far as personal ties went, not much. No family, nothing he could call home. He doubted seriously that the Houston boardinghouse where he'd spent the first twelve years of his life was still standing. He had a handful of good friends scattered around the world, but other than that, there was only Cass.

Cass Valenti. Small, dark, vivacious. And aggressive. Especially in bed. Ty grinned in reluctant remembrance. Cass was *not* a relaxing woman. They had absolutely nothing in common...except in bed.

For the better part of the past year, the crew had been working out of Wilmington, North Carolina. Tyrus had been lucky enough to find a fairly decent apartment ashore, and Cass had been his nearest neighbor. After the second day, she'd also been his lover.

The problem had come when he'd tried to tell her about the change in his situation. Armed with a fistful of literature and those damned pills, he'd had to wait for four days while she completed a concert tour with some guitar-playing kid in tight leather jeans. Cass worked for a public relations firm, and since the port city of Wilmington had been turned into Hollywood East by the location there of a major film studio, her career had soared.

There'd been plenty of time to go over all the strictures on diet and exercise while he waited. He'd even jogged a couple of miles the first day, feeling like an ass when a couple of commercial fishermen he knew called out a few ribald comments. From then on, he'd decided, if he had to run, he'd damned well do it in the middle of

the night, when no one could see him making a fool of
himself.

And he'd hit the salad bars, piling enough vegetation
onto his plate to feed an army of rabbits and then
smothering it with Italian dressing, and to hell with herbs
and lemon juice! If he was going to have to change his
whole eating pattern, he'd have to do it gradually. A man
had to have *some* pleasures. He'd planned to cut out salt
once his body got over the shock of being denied its usual
fare of broiled lobsters and thick rare steaks, well seasoned with things not on the damned list and washed
down with a couple of highballs. It was enough that he
had to load up on raw vegetables when the only ones he'd
ever eaten with any regularity were french fries and ko-
sher dills.

After the first few days on medication, his headaches
had left and hadn't returned. He'd figured he was on the
way to having the whole problem licked. Other than the
occasional drink, Ty had always taken excellent care of
himself, but hard, intensive work demanded equally intensive relaxation, and looking back, he admitted that
he'd been finding it increasingly hard to relax. The drinks
had slipped up on him. The fact that he'd been staring his
thirty-eighth birthday in the face hadn't helped.

For some time now he'd been aware of a growing feeling of restlessness, as if some vital element were missing
from his life. He'd started studying the men who flocked
to the beach with their families on weekends, the office
types who grew flabbier and balder each year, while their
women grew softer and thicker, and their families simply grew, until the five-year-old station wagon was
bursting at the seams.

On the whole they'd seemed surprisingly content with their lot, and for the life of him, Ty couldn't understand it. At his peak, he'd earned as much as two thousand dollars a day; he'd invested at least half of his earnings pretty wisely, he drove a car most men would sell their soul to possess, he'd spent his whole life doing precisely what he wanted to do—and he was worried about missing something? Hell! He had it made!

How many dreams had those poor fools surrendered to spend their life slogging away in some dull, safe job? If they were lucky, they got to spend two weeks a year at the beach with a wife who'd rather be shopping than fishing and a kid who'd rather be playing video games. For that they sacrificed?

Once when he'd been about twenty, he'd had a chance to stop off at Easter Island to see the monolithic heads left behind by some long-forgotten people. For years afterward, the memory had nagged at him. God, it had wiped him out, seeing those blind stone faces staring out to sea. Even then he'd felt as if they were trying to tell him something...but what the devil was it?

He still thought about them occasionally, more disturbed than he cared to admit by something that lurked just beyond the limits of his understanding. Dammit! Why should a bunch of stone faces—or some shoe salesman on a weekend trip to the beach with his family, for that matter—make him feel as if he were missing some vital element in his life?

A few drinks usually helped when he got too restless. Or a weekend with a woman. While he'd waited, panic-stricken, for Cass to get back to town, he'd done without the comfort of either.

She'd returned from her tour full of enthusiasm. Resigned to letting her wind down at her own rate, Ty had watched indulgently while she pirouetted about the apartment, high on her own energy, full of ideas for promoting her tight-panted rock singer and herself along with him.

At last she'd whirled onto his lap, throwing her arms around his neck. "And he's just the beginning! What do you think, Ty? With the studios expanding all over the place, every hopeful east of the Mississippi will be trooping down here waiting to be discovered. I think I'll just skim off the cream of the crop before anyone else even gets a shot at it, and then maybe move to Nashville, or even Hollywood. I'm thinking of getting out of P.R. and going into management."

"What do you know about managing?" Ty had scoffed, accustomed to Cass's mercurial moods. It was that same excitability, combined with a streak of shrewd practicality, that made her so good at her job. "I thought your forté was creating camera opportunities and finagling free media coverage."

"My forté is people, and that includes dealing, negotiating, ego massaging, and playing a lot of ball. So what else do you think a manager does?"

"At the moment, it's not your managerial talents that interest me, honey." He'd found that certain place at the back of her knee that drove her wild.

"And what are you particularly interested in at the moment?" Eyes glittering under silver-blue lids, she'd wriggled closer, all the while making those soft, guttural sounds at the back of her throat that always turned him on, and Ty had felt the familiar response stirring in his loins. "He's crazy about me, you know. A nineteen-year-old kid, with groupies practically ripping his clothes off every time the bus slows down, and he couldn't keep his eyes or his hands off me.''

"Hands, too, huh?" Ty knew what she was up to. Cass enjoyed measuring her importance on a yardstick of jealousy, but at the moment he was too busy with buttons and buckles to play along.

"Aren't you jealous? Did you miss me? Tell me how much you missed me," Cass had demanded. Game number two. Cass loved games.

The two weeks of abstinence were telling on him. "How about a hands-on demonstration, instead?" he'd growled, scooping her up in his arms and carrying her into the bedroom they shared whenever both happened to be in town at the same time.

"Damn!" Tyrus swore now, remembering. He wiped away a drop of water that had struck his shoulder and continued to prowl the rose-sprigged bedroom, resenting the fact that it was not that other bedroom, the one with the garish blue carpet, the plastic-veneer furniture, and the woman who made all those things seem irrelevant.

Another drop struck the ornate iron bed, spattered, and was absorbed by the ivory candlewick bedspread. He ignored it. He ignored the drumming rain outside, the scuffling sounds that still came from overhead. Smacking a hard fist into the palm of his hand, he relished the sting of flesh against flesh as he relived the memory of his first ignominious failure. And the failures that had come after that.

Impotent!

Oh, sure, it was the medication—at least that was what the doc had told him. But when he'd quit taking the damned stuff, things hadn't gotten any better. Cass had accused him of a number of unflattering things, the least of which had been unfaithfulness.

"When the devil would I have had time?" he'd demanded. "I told you I was offshore for a solid week, and then this blood-pressure thing hit me. When the hell do you think I had either the time or the inclination to go cruising for another woman?"

"Well, I don't know about the time, sweetie, but you sure have lost your inclination. Poor baby, I've heard about this sort of thing happening to men when they approach middle age. Tell me, do you have hot flashes, too?"

Soggy corduroy squelched as Anny crawled along the narrow plank that traversed ceiling joints, insulation, wiring conduit, and the dust of more than a hundred years. There *had* to be a better way than this. If she couldn't afford to replace the roof, maybe she should settle for having the attic floored. First, of course, she'd have to find a carpenter willing to work in a crawlspace that could be reached only by climbing a homemade ladder and squeezing through a narrow access door.

By the dim light of a single forty-watt bulb, she inched toward the opening, trying not to slosh the water over the rim of the plastic bucket. Her knees were already raw, her spine was painfully bent, and if she lifted her head to ease her back, she'd probably crack her skull on a rafter.

For the third time, one knee caught on the sagging hem of her baggy sweater, almost causing her to fall on her face. The bucket tipped and water splashed on her rain-drenched clothing.

"Beans!" Lowering the bucket carefully, Anny sat on her heels and peeled the wet, cotton-knit garment over her head, tossing it at the doorway just as a head and a pair of wide shoulders appeared there.

Tyrus's temper shot skyward. Undraping his face, he fought it down to a manageable level. "Would you mind telling me just what the hell you're doing up here?" he seethed.

"What does it look like?" Anny snapped back. Having just hit her surly tenant in the face, she covered her embarrassment with irritation. "I'm scrubbing the inside of the ceiling!"

"My bedroom's leaking."

"Tough. Would you mind not blocking the light?" she retorted coolly, momentarily forgetting the fact that she was clad in no more than a wet nylon bra and a pair of clinging wet corduroy jeans. Her nose was already twitching, thanks to all the dust. Any minute now she'd begin to sneeze, and once she started, she would be helpless. Fourteen in a row was her record.

Ty's gaze narrowed, his pupils adjusting quickly to the dim light. Strange she might be; strange she undoubtedly was, but had he really thought her unattractive? She had the sort of understated beauty that didn't register right away, and he blinked and then looked again. For some reason, he was reminded of the first time he'd been shown Canis Major as a boy. It had taken a long time to locate the constellation at first, but after that it seemed to jump out at him each time he lifted his eyes.

As the silence grew thicker, Anny shifted awkwardly on her abused knees. "Look, I'm sorry I hit you with my sweater, but how was I to know you'd show up at the wrong time? I didn't even know you knew where the attic was.''

A cold drip struck the lower part of her spine, and she stiffened. Reaching behind her, she wiped at the wetness, and the touch of her heated skin reminded her that she wasn't exactly dressed for receiving. "This is embarrassing," she grumbled. It was her ill temper that embarrassed her far more than her shirtlessness. She'd grown up seeing her father's models in every state of undress as he draped, pinned, scowled, and sketched, but rudeness was not normally one of her failings.

Tyrus found himself studying with growing interest the woman who crouched some ten feet away, her short, pale brown hair plastered to a set of remarkably fine cheekbones, breasts swaying above a sapling-slender waist like two small, ripe pears.

"I thought maybe you were squirreling away a winter's supply of nuts up here." His deep voice registered considerably less than its usual abrasiveness.

"Look, would you mind letting me get on with it? If you have a complaint about your leaky ceiling, I'll meet you downstairs when I'm done here, okay?" Under other circumstances, Anny would have willingly accepted the olive branch, if that's what it was, but at the moment her bones were protesting and her nose was itching.

"Maybe a relay would help. You slide it halfway, I'll meet you and get it down the ladder. Where do I empty it?"

Anny didn't even hesitate; *anything* to shorten the agony. "I'd better warn you, there are still two more to go after this one, but if you don't mind, you can empty them in your bathtub. Sorry, again, but it's the handiest place."

"No problem." Tyrus hung her sweater from a projecting rung of the ladder, climbed another rung, then eased one knee onto the plank. "Not much room up here, is there?" he asked, his shoulders scraping the two-by-fours that framed in the opening.

"I think this space is supposed to be for ventilation or something." Anny edged closer, shoving the bucket before her. "I just wish they'd vented it under the eaves instead of right through the roof."

"You need a new roof," Ty observed sagely, leaning forward to take the bucket from her.

"Why do you think *you're* here?" Cautiously, she began her backward trek along the splintery plank. There was no room to turn around.

"Temporary insanity's the best I can come up with." He inched back toward the opening. Anny heard him swear as his head cracked into a rafter, then swear again as his elbows struck the door facing when he tried to lift the bucket through the narrow opening. Pursing her lips, she struggled against the grin that threatened. "At least there aren't any bats up here," he observed grudgingly.

"Not this time of evening, anyway. They're all out to dinner."

"Oh, God, not those, too," Ty groaned. Moving as carefully as he could, he managed to descend the ladder without spilling more than a few pints of water. "Which room is directly under this thing?" he called back.

"Did you spill it? Don't worry, I always spill it going down the ladder, too. It's over the living room, but it doesn't drip through because when the bees came back, they moved into the space between the floors. It's all beeswax and honey in there."

With one hand on the knob of the door that opened into the upstairs hallway, Tyrus halted, shook his head, then moved on again. "I don't believe this," he said softly. "I'll wake up in a little while and find out I've dreamed the whole thing. There are no rats in the freezer. There are no bees in the floorboards. There's no half-naked woman shifting buckets of water around in the attic. Dreams of a starving man—that's all this is."

He emptied the bucket into the claw-footed bathtub and returned for another one. Eyeing the satiny brown wood of the wall-mounted ladder distrustfully, he considered returning to his room and leaving her to finish the job alone.

Halfway along the attic, nursing along another overflowing bucket, Anny greeted him with a smile that did remarkable things to her features. "How'd you know I was up here, anyway?"

Resigned to finishing what he'd started, Tyrus tossed her the empty bucket and eased his shoulders through the doorway. "From the dust that kept falling in my face," he grunted. "Not to mention the noise. I thought maybe you were up here trapping unwary rodents."

"I should have mentioned the leaks. There's just one more bucket after this, but I can handle it if you want to go on with whatever you were doing."

"I was *trying* to brood, but never mind, I'll get back to it later."

They met halfway along the plank, and Ty's hands closed over the sides of the bucket, inadvertently squeezing so that water overflowed the top. He looked up to apologize for his carelessness and cracked the back of his head on a sharp-edged rafter.

"Oh, I'm so sorry," Anny crooned to the accompaniment of his extremely proficient cursing. "Look, why don't you just get on with your brooding and leave this for me to finish up? I'm used to it. Honestly, I haven't knocked myself out in years."

Combing his fingers through his hair, Ty estimated the damage. No bleeding, at least. He fingered the rising lump and scowled. "Just give me the damned bucket and let's get on with it. I won't get much sleep with mud dripping onto my face."

Silently, Anny retreated along the plank, watching his hunched shoulders as they blocked the light from the bulb over the doorway. Sleep? What happened to his brooding? Besides, it was barely dark yet; she hadn't even had her dinner. Somehow, she wouldn't have sized him up as an early-to-bed, early-to-rise type. A double-ended-candle burner would be more like it. Those heavy-lidded eyes, the mouth that so fascinated her even when it was curled in derision... Those were not the features of an ascetic.

Turning sideways, she braced herself with one hand along a ceiling joist and reached out for the bucket that was wedged under the eaves. Prying it loose was going to be awkward, for it was completely full. She was distracted by Tyrus's return.

Anny's experience with men wasn't all that extensive—in fact, it could hardly even be called experience. Nevertheless, every female hormone in her body had reacted with alarming enthusiasm to her first sight of Tyrus Clay. It had taken all the prudence and pragmatism she possessed to enable her to ignore his presence in her house this past week.

Dammit, this one was being stubborn! Wedged by its weight between the joists, it had to be lifted and then eased carefully toward her. And as if that weren't enough, halfway there it had to be lifted over the wiring conduit.

Knees spread apart for balance, she braced herself and tucked her hands under the wire handle, lifting just enough to clear the lead pipe that encased the electrical wiring. Straining muscles quivered as slowly, carefully, she drew the plastic bucket to her, her eyes focused on the shivering surface of the water that threatened to overflow its sides. It was just as she turned to place her burden carefully beside her on the plank that the handle pulled loose.

"Oh, no!" she wailed. Five gallons of cold water flowed over her lap, over the joists, soaking into batts of insulation and threatening whole communities of mud-daubers' tunnels.

Bending from the waist, Anny crossed her arms on the dripping plank and buried her face, giving way to noisy sobs of pure frustration. It was several moments before she felt the hand on her head, a moment more before she felt the soft, warm breath stirring the hair against her wet cheeks.

"Go away," she said, chokingly. "There's not room for two people up here."

Tyrus was acutely aware of that fact, but he could hardly have turned his back and left her there bawling her eyes out over a lousy bucket of water. Still, he might not have acted quite so quixotically if he'd known how she was going to affect him at close range—the clean, wild-flower scent of her skin and her hair, the heat eddying around her body as she knelt in the gloomy attic, face down, bottom up.

"Come on, honey, it's nothing to cry over. Not even spilled milk—just a little water. Come on downstairs now and let me make you some coffee, all right?"

"Don't mind me, Tyrus," Anny sniffled. "I always fall apart over trifles. It k-keeps me from c-catching colds."

Ty, his hand hovering helplessly just above her naked shoulder, lifted his eyes to the dripping rafters overhead. The rain, if anything, had increased.

She cried to keep from catching colds. Tyrus sighed. It had finally gotten to him, then. He'd gone to the doctor with a simple headache and ended up in the sort of place where they put women like Anny Cousins.

Three

I always cry over little things,'' Anny sobbed.

"That's crazy," Tyrus retorted gruffly. Tentatively, he lowered his hand, jerking it away at the first touch of her warm, silky flesh. It would be a damned sight easier to offer a little friendly comfort if she had on more clothes.

"No, it's not," she argued, sniffing noisily as she struggled to get herself under control. "It's healthy to cry over little things."

If he'd needed something to bring him down, it took only this small reminder that his landlady was slightly peculiar—to put it charitably. "There, there," he mumbled, embarrassed for her, for himself, and already wondering how quickly he could get himself out of his lease.

On the other hand, it was reassuring to know that his body still reacted to the sight of an attractive, scantily clothed woman the way nature intended it should. Under other circumstances, he might be tempted to explore the situation a bit further. "Come on, dry off and I'll make you the best cup of coffee you've ever tasted, okay? Feel better now?"

By the time Anny joined him in the kitchen, she'd showered and changed into dry clothes and a pair of Hannibal's wool boot socks. Her hair clung darkly to her head, for she hadn't taken time to dry it. In fact, she wasn't at all sure he'd be waiting for her. For someone who made such a big noise about privacy and nonintervention, Tyrus was acting decidedly out of character tonight.

"I make it strong," he said by way of greeting. "You might need to water yours down." Actually, coffee, strong or otherwise, was the last thing he needed at this time of night. He had trouble enough falling asleep as it was.

"I'm starved. I walked at least five miles this afternoon with a full load. You probably had dinner before you came home, but I haven't had a bite since lunch."

"I usually get by on one meal in the middle of the day," Tyrus admitted. And he'd sell his soul right now for a rare steak about two inches thick, loaded with everything that stupid diet sheet forbade.

"Dieting? You don't look like the type." Anny opened the refrigerator to browse, and Ty gazed apprehensively at the freezer compartment over her head. He made up his mind swiftly; if it came out of a can, he'd eat it. If it came out of that freezer, no *way*!

"Sure you won't change your mind?"

Ty allowed his gaze to skim down the colorless, shapeless thing she'd put on to the woolen socks that ex-

tended several inches beyond her toes. He was hungry, all
right. It was a perennial condition. If he took her up on
her offer, it would have nothing to do with any interest in
the subtle curves of her body. "I reckon I could stand a
bite of something or other before I turn in," he allowed.

"How about a baked potato loaded with cheese and
bacon and onions and anything else I can come up with?'
Anny suggested, rounding up ingredients and placing
them on a scrubbed wooden table beside the week's mail.

Ty's stomach rolled over noisily. "Bacon, cheese, and
onion will be fine for me," he put in hastily. He was
hungry, all right, but he refused to eat anything he
couldn't readily identify—not when it came from the
kitchen of his eccentric landlady. "But no extra salt," he
added reluctantly. The cheese and bacon were off limits,
too, but he was cutting *down*, not *out*. Until he got things
patched up again with Cass, he lacked the motivation to
go cold turkey.

While Anny moved about the kitchen with an efficiency that belied her languorous appearance, Ty wandered about the house, examining the overflowing
bookshelves and the framed photos that covered a whole
wall. It had probably been a mistake to drop his guard
this way, he mused. What if she started something? It was
a hell of a lot easier to let a lady down if he'd never shared
a meal with her.

The snapshots obviously spanned several generations.
There was one of an old man and a younger Anny in
bibbed overalls and a straw hat, another of his landlady
standing between a couple who might have stepped off
the pages of a high-fashion magazine.

Examining the photo more closely, he grinned. He
didn't know who the devil they were, but he'd never seen

a more mismatched trio: Anny in another of her bag-lady costumes, arms crossed over her chest, and the accompanying pair looking grimly cheerful.

There were several pictures of men, a couple of Anny with the same man, and another of the same guy with another woman. A brother? Could be. For the first time, it occurred to him to wonder about her life's circumstances. She didn't seem to go out much, and there'd been no visitors as far as he knew. She might be married. Separated? Divorced?

Hell, it was no concern of his. He turned away, frowning.

Still, he couldn't help but wonder about her, living all alone out here in the boonies with a freezer full of mice and an attic full of buckets. He'd always enjoyed the company of women, and under normal circumstances he might even enjoy getting to know this one.

But this one was different, he reminded himself...in more ways than one. In his previous relationships with women, there'd been an unspoken understanding that sex, with no strings attached, was a prime objective.

"It's on the table," Anny called out, breaking into his thoughts.

Later on, as he watched her dig into her enormous baked potato with a remarkable lack of self-consciousness, he reminded himself once more that Anny Cousins was hardly his type. Besides which, he was in no shape to start something he couldn't finish.

"More cheese? I grated lots of it. How about some—"

"No, this is just fine," he said hurriedly, loading his fork with bacon, melted cheese, and steaming potato. It had been a bad idea from the start. He was inviting something he wasn't sure he wanted to continue. Not to mention the fact that he was establishing a precedent. Rather than dine alone on the sort of foods he was supposed to eat, he'd managed to wean himself from an evening meal altogether. After tonight, his stomach was going to be giving him hell every evening about this time.

"Have you always lived around here?" Increasingly uncomfortable under her candid gaze, he asked the question, telling himself he owed her a certain amount of polite conversation in return for the meal.

"No, not always. For about ten years, though."

"Family come from these parts?"

"My mother's family. Great-uncle Hannibal left me the house."

Tyrus nodded and attacked his potato again. As big as it was, he could have handled two more.

"How about you? I didn't ask what you do at Duke. You're probably not an Egyptologist, though, are you?"

He stared at her blankly. "An Egyptologist? Am I supposed to be?"

Anny shrugged and helped herself to another strip of bacon, munching daintily between huge bites of potato. "Your name," she explained, licking the cheese from her lips. When he continued to stare at her, she elaborated. "Tyrus, papyrus. Clay, as in clay tablets."

"I see. You always size people up that way?"

"Usually I don't bother to size them up at all, but if they're going to live with me, it's different. It's only because of the roof, you know. Well, maybe the foundation, too, but that doesn't show. At least you're not a dinosaur."

Shaking his head, Ty shot a glance at the freezer and then turned back to his landlady again. Damned if he wasn't halfway intrigued, in spite of himself. The woman spoke a language all her own. It sounded familiar; he recognized the words. So how come nothing she said made sense? If those damned pills had addled his wits, too, then that medic was going to need every cent of malpractice insurance he could afford.

"Uh—" He hesitated, at a loss to know how to converse with someone whose logic defied all the rules.

"Tyrannosaurus. You know, Tyrus? *Ty*-rannosau-*rus*? Dinosaur?"

Ty nodded obligingly. He'd agree with everything she said, finish his meal, and then get the hell out of there before she started to make sense to him. If that ever happened, he'd know for sure that he was around the bend! Diligently, he scraped the last of the cheese from his plate.

"You haven't been having breakfast here, have you? That was a part of the deal. I usually negotiate kitchen privileges *after* I've looked my tenant over." Anny licked her lips and smiled confidently, her brown eyes wide and candid. "You know how it is—some people you really wouldn't want messing around in your kitchen."

Ty choked on his coffee, and she leaned over and thumped him firmly on the back. "Okay, okay," he gasped, tipping the mug to empty it down his raw throat.

"Good. Well, all I wanted to say was that if you'd like to fix your own supper here, too, it's all right with me. You seem harmless enough."

He seemed harmless! Hopelessly bemused now, Ty shook his head. "Are you by any chance a witch?"

Was he implying that she was bewitching? Anny fluffed her hair, wishing she'd taken the time to dry it. To be on the safe side, she'd better take him literally. "Sorry to disappoint you. Nothing so exotic, I'm afraid. I'm just an ordinary commercial artist.''

A commercial artist? Come to think of it, she'd mentioned a studio that first day. ''What sort of work do you do?'' So much for his intention to eat and run. But commercial artist or not, if a black cat should happen to stroll in, he was packing his bags.

''I illustrate books for a small publisher in Charlotte and free-lance for a couple of regional magazines. I've been thinking of doing a regional coloring book with a historical slant if I can talk my editor into publishing it. And maybe an owl-and-hawk book.''

Which was as good an opening as he was likely to find, Ty decided. ''Have you…uh…got a cat? I haven't seen one around here.''

''You're not allergic, are you? I don't have one, but if you're allergic to fur, you might be allergic to feathers, too.''

''The…uh…mice in the freezer? Something to do with your artwork?''

Anny stood and took both plates, stacking them carelessly on the drainboard. ''Oh, that's my hobby,'' she explained. ''Want to finish the coffee, or will it keep you awake?''

Ty allowed her to refill his mug. His chances of sleeping were practically nil, anyway. ''Your hobby is freezing mice?'' he persisted in a mild tone.

''Come on into the living room so I won't have to wash the dishes,'' Anny invited, and he followed her, sinking deeper and deeper under a spell he didn't even try to understand.

Comfortably ensconced on the sofa, her outsized flannel shirt billowing out around her, Anny explained both the demands and the fascination of incubating deserted eggs, raising orphaned owls, and rehabilitating injured ones.

Tyrus listened while his gaze strayed over her face. No makeup he knew of could be responsible for the length of those lashes, the perfect arch of those brows. Cass would sooner have told her real age than let any man see her bare-faced and wet-headed.

"The only bad part is the pigeons. I have a friend who helps me out by supplying them when I have babies—the protein content is terrific. Once they're old enough to go out, I put them in a baby bathtub in the mews and start them on bits of mice. That's where the frozen ones come in. As they get older, I train them to pounce by using a wad of paper on a string, and then we start with live mice."

"I hope your shots are up to date." He had to admire her spunk. The women he knew would have climbed the wall at the mere mention of bits of mice. There was a faint covering of freckles that gave her skin a velvety look. He wondered how it would feel to his touch.

"Naturally, I get bitten occasionally. So do my babies, but it's amazing how fast they learn to hunt. Instinct. The real problem is imprinting. It's fatal, you know."

Look at her, Ty mused...no style, no makeup, going on about owls and mice and pigeons as though she weren't a young, attractive woman alone with a man.

"With a single, there's no choice. It'll either be a pet or go to a small zoo somewhere—it can never make it in the wild."

Could women tell about those things? What was that business he'd read somewhere about pheromones? Was there some hidden signal a man sent off that let them know they were safe? God, if that was so... No, that was impossible. Cass hadn't guessed beforehand, and what Cass didn't know about the opposite sex wasn't worth knowing.

"I've even tried a mask and gloves, but I'm not sure that method works. The only thing to do is to get them into the mews as early as possible. Would you like to see my mews? Or is it mew? You know, I've never known if that's plural or singular—someday I'll look it up. I built it out of scrap lumber, so it's rough, but the owls don't seem to mind. You have to have one before you can be licensed, you know."

Dismissing his unsettling doubts, Ty relaxed under the open warmth that shone from those wide brown eyes. Her wackiness was contagious. "Yeah, I'd like that," he said, not particularly interested in whatever it was she'd built from scrap lumber. "Now that you've explained about those frozen mice."

Anny squirmed into a more comfortable position, tucking one foot under her. "Sorry about that. By the way, if you need a blender, use the one in the upper left-hand cabinet, not the one in the pantry."

Easing his long legs under the coffee table, Tyrus encountered two pairs of shoes and a magazine. "Thanks— I'll manage without a blender. You might consider posting a warning for your next guest, though. I reached for a tray of ice and saw those things and—"

"That's why you thought I might be a witch?" She laughed. "Sorry to disappoint you. I almost wish I were. If I could cast spells, I'd cast one to stop the leaks, and another one to shore up my foundation before the kitchen breaks away from the rest of the house. I keep saving up the money and then spending it on something else.''

His eyes dropped once more to the soft flannel that shrouded a body he knew for a fact to be worth exhibiting, and Ty wondered why she didn't spend a few bucks on herself. In a pair of well-fitting jeans and a decent top—maybe one of those sleeveless things Cass wore—she'd be a class act.

His imagination took flight, inflamed by too many weeks of celibacy, and Ty shifted uncomfortably. Rising, he turned to glance down at her upturned face. ''I'd better turn in,'' he murmured. Her lips parted when she lifted her chin to meet his gaze, and Ty cleared his throat and looked away. ''Thanks for the dinner, Anny. It hit the spot.''

Anny watched him move toward the stairs. ''I owed you for the help with those buckets. Next time I'll empty them before they get so full. Good night, Tyrus.''

Long after he'd disappeared up the stairs, his image lingered in her mind. He was a strange man. Marvelous to look at, probably fascinating to talk to if he ever opened up. And not nearly as awful as he'd tried to make her believe. Something was bothering him. One minute they'd been relaxed and chatting away like old friends, and the next thing she knew he was tensing up, as though she'd said something to offend him. Or embarrass him?

Looking back, Anny couldn't think of a single thing she'd said that would bring about that look of acute discomfort. It couldn't be the mice; he understood about those now—and she understood those furtive glances at her freezer compartment.

For a long time after she went to bed, Anny allowed her thoughts to linger on Tyrus Clay. He was unlike any retired professor she'd ever known. Hannibal had been a professor emeritus of religious philosophy, and certainly no two men could have been more different.

Who *was* Tyrus Clay? What was he *doing* here? There was something untamed about the man, something that reminded her of the injured peregrine falcon she'd had in her care for a short period. He was nothing at all like other men she'd known. Not that there'd been that many, in spite of the efforts of matchmaking friends.

Ten years ago, newly graduated, hopeful, and beginning to pick up a few decent commissions from local advertisers, she'd moved in with Hannibal, thinking it would be a temporary situation. At twenty-four, she'd held out hope for meeting that one special man.

By the time she'd reached the age of thirty-four, she'd come to accept her single life-style, having found most men, including the one she'd been engaged to for three years, lacking some vital element. Hannibal had spoiled her for lesser men. Their friendship had been based on a similarity of values, an insatiable curiosity about the world and its creatures, and a true delight in exploring and examining whatever lay within reach.

He'd taught her to appreciate each day for the unique treasures it brought, and now she had everything a woman could want: a home and an interesting career, vigorous health, and a circle of friends that included several old beaux...as well as the women they'd later married.

Ironically, she was even godmother to the six-year-old son of her ex-fiancé. Sid had been an assistant professor of zoology at Chapel Hill and she'd been a senior when they'd met. They'd dated a year, been engaged for two, and then he'd met a giddy little freshman and married her within the month. Anny had been one of the bridesmaids.

She prided herself on never having lost a boyfriend. If one after the other they fell in love and married some-one else, so what? They still remained her friends. Now and then they visited her to show off the latest offspring, and Anny played aunt to a growing number of babies. She might occasionally wish that a few of them were her own, but she could honestly say that her heart had never been broken by any man.

It was several days before Anny saw her boarder again. She'd seen evidence of his having used the kitchen to make coffee, and once there was a paper sack in her trash bearing the logo of a fast-food franchise. For a man who looked so vitally healthy, his eating habits seemed a little strange, but it was no business of hers. She hadn't taken him in to raise.

"Your car's getting plastered with oak leaves," she observed. She'd come home early when a cold northeast wind had sprung up, having forgotten her jacket again. "Do you need another blanket on your bed?"

Tyrus had been about to sample the alfalfa sprouts he'd picked up on the way home. He'd heard one of the marine biology students telling another that his wife kept them on hand for him, swearing that they were better than the fabled raw oysters. "Have you ever eaten these things?" he asked suspiciously, poking at the crisp, tightly packed threads.

"Sure. I like wheat sprouts better, though. They're sweeter." Anny slid her knapsack off onto the table and propped her metal detector in a corner. "You're home early, aren't you?"

"No reason to hang around the campus," Ty replied morosely. "I've got a stack of reading to do, and I may as well do it here. Looks as if it might rain again, and that road of yours is treacherous enough under the best conditions." He glanced at the metal detector. "Lost something?"

"Lost something?" she repeated blankly.

"The detector. Most people borrow them to find a ring or a set of keys, don't they?" A grin creased his lean cheeks, and he leaned back against the doorframe. "Or were you searching for buried treasure?"

"Buried treasure, by all means. Did you know about all the trade routes that crisscrossed this area for hundreds of years? It was practically a main thoroughfare long before Durham was even thought of."

"That explains all those treasure-hunting magazines under your coffee table." Ty could remember the fever. He'd once burned with it, too, as had every salvage diver he'd ever known. His personal dream had been a Spanish privateer that had gone down in the early sixteenth century. The last thing he'd expected was to find a strain of the same fever up here in the foothill country at the back of beyond.

"If you like, I'll show you my relics after I get a fire going and start something for supper. Have you eaten yet?" Anny struggled out from under the tangle of straps that crisscrossed her body and hung her camera, binoculars, and knapsack on assorted doorknobs. She looked expectantly at Ty, waiting for his answer.

"I'd planned to sample that stuff." He nodded disgustedly toward the carton of sprouts.

"Why?"

"Why?" he repeated.

"Why would any grown man in his right mind settle for grazing instead of having a decent meal? You can't maintain your strength on carbohydrates alone, you know."

Without quite knowing how it came about, Tyrus found himself some two hours later sharing the sofa with her while they pored over local history books, treasure-hunting magazines, and compared notes on various models of metal detectors. Hers was about as sophisticated and as expensive as they came, and if the results were anything to go by, she was thoroughly checked out on it.

"All this stuff came from a mill, you say?" He examined the odd-shaped scrap of rusty metal thoughtfully.

"The river around here was practically lined with them. This was Occaneechi Indian country after they got chased down here from the Virginia border by the English. That was in 1676, and they died out less than a hundred years later—no one knows exactly why, but sometimes I feel almost like a trespasser on their river, in their forests."

Anny, her eyes gleaming softly in the lamplight, turned to face him, drawing her feet up onto the couch to warm them with her hands. They'd built a fire in the fireplace, but the old house was drafty.

Tyrus felt her feet brush against his thigh. The strength of his physical response jolted him—which didn't mean a single thing, as he'd already learned to his acute embarrassment. He'd responded to Cass in the usual way, too, and that had been the end of it.

"Of course, if you're not a history buff, you'll probably find it all pretty boring."

Anny wasn't his type. Besides, he already had a woman. Cass would come to her senses once he'd beat this hypertension thing. "I'm not at all bored," he assured her, taking the fragment of rusty iron and examining it with every evidence of interest. What the devil; it sure beat lying up there in the dark wondering what Cass was doing, who she was sleeping with, and how long it would be before he could call himself a man again.

The foot burrowed against his hip again, like a kitten looking for a warm lap, and Ty squirmed, feeling the heat from the fireplace to an uncomfortable degree. Anny was as screwball as they came, he reminded himself forcefully. Great to look at, fascinating to listen to, but definitely not the sort of woman a man wanted to get mixed up with, even under normal circumstances.

His hand closed over her icy toes, and he began to chaff them between fingers and thumb. "That thing really puts out the heat, doesn't it?" He ran a finger under his collar as he eyed the small brick fireplace. He had a one-track mind these days. Let him so much as touch a woman and he started envisioning all sorts of forbidden delights.

Not forbidden—impossible! Which was a damned sight worse.

He snatched his hand away. What was he trying to do? Make a fool of himself all over again? Being ridiculed by a woman—*any* woman—was pretty hard to take. Why invite it?

"You never told me what you did before you came to Duke," Anny reminded him.

"I'm a diver. *Was* a diver," he corrected shortly.

"Have you ever done any treasure diving?" Anny wriggled herself into a cross-legged position beside him and leaned forward, interest lending a breathless look to her rather ordinary face.

"Yeah, I guess I did my share before I grew up. Off the Keys, mostly."

She continued to gaze at him expectantly, noting the slight ridge in an otherwise straight nose, the thrusting jaw, the level deepset eyes. "You sound as if you don't approve of it," she observed after a few moments.

Ty stroked the late-day stubble on his chin. When he dropped his hand, it came to rest on her toes again, and with a wry grin, he continued his warming massage. "I guess I didn't like what it did to me. After a couple of years I realized that it was a sickness. I wasn't even certified back then, and I was taking all sorts of chances just to be in on the kill. Gold fever. I used to read about it when I was young…Jack London, the Gold Rush days. Treasure fever—it's all the same. I didn't like what I was becoming, so I got out." His palm slipped down to the arch of her foot, and he felt her unconscious reaction, heard the slight catch of her breath. God, she was all silk and nerves! What sort of woman was hiding behind that scrubbed face, the drab, shapeless clothes?

Conscious of a warm glow of pleasure that came from a stimulating exchange of ideas, Anny considered his words. In a broad sense, she understood exactly what he meant. Hadn't she opted to get out of a situation that was no good for her? Wouldn't any rational person? "I think maybe I inherited my strain from my great-uncle. He was an armchair adventurer—all these books made up for all the places he couldn't go, the things he couldn't do. He was terribly crippled with arthritis when he died, but he never lost that sense of…of excitement, of discovery."

She sighed, her eyes focused on a time and place Tyrus couldn't share. And then she brightened again. "You know, I think I'd like some hot tea with lots of milk. What about you?"

Hot tea. With *milk*, yet. If Cass could see him now, she'd laugh herself sick. Playing footsie with a freckle-faced female who lacked even the most basic of womanly wiles, and drinking tea with milk instead of...

Bitterness curled inside him again, and he fought against it. By this time, they'd have been back from dinner. He'd have poured a nightcap, and Cass would be dancing, arms extended invitingly. Cass had to have background noise. The first thing she did on entering a room was to turn on the tape player. She'd do her best to persuade him to dance with her, and after a twelve-hour workday, he'd be wondering when she'd wind down enough to go to bed.

"Yeah, tea sounds great," he heard himself saying. Surprisingly enough, it did.

Four

For the next week Tyrus was scrupulously polite on the few occasions when his path happened to cross Anny's. His schooling had been sporadic, at best, and he seemed to spend all his time reading to catch up on theory. His eyes were tired, his temper increasingly short, and the miserable light in his room was worse than useless. He'd give everything he owned to be able to dive into a choppy sea and swim until he was exhausted.

At first Anny was puzzled by his coolness. The night they'd shared a pot of tea and talked until all hours had been one of the most enjoyable she'd spent in years. Still, she rationalized, some people were like that; blow hot, blow cold. Friends one day, strangers again the next.

Taking advantage of a run of good weather, she did the last of the fall season's field drawings for the nature-walk book she was illustrating. She'd have until the first snowfall to turn them into the finished product, and then she'd be ready to start on the final group, depicting the dormant period. The timing on this particular commission had worked out perfectly. She'd agreed to start on illustrations for a children's adventure book as soon as the author could provide a rough draft.

Tyrus confronted her at the door as she hurried up the back steps. She'd walked four miles to capture a certain stand of silky-leather beeches, with their curly, clematis-like seed heads. "About my reading light," he greeted her abruptly.

"Hang on until I unload my gear, will you? I've got to see about getting myself a donkey if I keep on at this rate," Anny panted. She'd jogged the last mile, camera and binoculars flapping, knapsack flopping, metal detector growing heavier by the minute. "What about it?" she asked, easing the crepe-soled boots first from one tired foot, then the other.

"Hmm?" Distracted by the flush of color that warmed her dramatic cheekbones, Ty allowed his gaze to travel downward to where her breasts thrust prominently between a multitude of crisscrossed straps.

"Your light," Anny reminded him. "Here, untangle me from these things, will you?" In trying to remove the knapsack first, she'd almost strangled herself with the other straps.

His hands, cool, dry, and hard, brushed against her throat. Barely recovered from the exertion of running that last uphill mile, Anny's heart slammed into her rib cage again. She swallowed hard and looked away while he unburdened her. How could she have forgotten the effect he had on her? After not seeing him for days, it was stronger than ever. He must have had his batteries on "charge" all week.

"Law on your tail?" Ty drawled as he eased the pack from her back.

Anny tugged off a camel-tan stocking cap that matched her hair perfectly, sending the electrified strands flying. She unwound the matching knit scarf from her neck and tossed it over a chair back. "Sometimes I run just because I can. You know, like the mountain?"

Eyes crinkling into a reluctant grin, Ty extricated her from the last of the straps and leaned against the doorjamb. "Sometimes you run just because you can. Like the mountain," he repeated thoughtfully. "Did you ever stop to listen to yourself when you talk, Anny? You don't make a whole lot of sense, you know."

Pausing in the act of washing her hands in the sink, she glanced over her shoulder. "I don't? Well, I suppose it's possible. Comes from living alone and talking to myself. I seldom bother to listen to what I'm saying. Are you hungry? I've got some country ham I can fry. Would you like a few eggs to go with it?"

Ty's imagination conjured up a platter of ham, grits, and red-eye gravy. Country ham. Fried, salty, completely off limits. He was as hungry as a bear. "Maybe an egg," he temporized.

"Ham and eggs for two, okay? You can make the coffee. What's the matter? Is your bulb burned out?" She bent over the sink to splash water over her face, completely missing the look of consternation that crossed his face.

Recovering quickly, Ty allowed his gaze to follow the line of her long, slender legs from their shapely source down to a pair of rumpled woolen socks. Funny, he'd never thought of corduroy as being particularly seductive before. "My bulb," he muttered. "Yeah, well, I do a lot of reading, and there's not a lamp in my room that puts out a decent light. I thought if you had a floor lamp you weren't using, I might borrow it while I'm here."

Anny disappeared into the pantry and returned with a mummified country ham. While he watched, she took down a lethal-looking knife and proceeded to sever four slices.

"Pretty salty, huh?" Another of his favorites joined the list of past pleasures: anchovies, salted peanuts, caviar, country ham...

Laying the slices aside, Anny slathered a thick coat of shortening over the cut to reseal it and returned the ham to the pantry. "Peanut-fed, pepper-cured, corncob-smoked, and aged almost two years. A farmer friend of Uncle Hannibal's gave it to me last Christmas."

"Maybe I'd better pass on the ham. An egg, maybe a couple of scrambled eggs, though..."

"You don't like country ham? We'll make it bacon, then."

"Just the eggs." Ty wondered why he hadn't simply asked for the lamp and gone back upstairs. "Matter of fact, I'm trying to cut down on salt."

So now she'd know, he thought miserably. Every magazine on the newsstands seemed to be running headlines on the relationship between hypertension drugs and impotence; the prime reason to cut down on salt was hypertension. Hell, he might as well be wearing the scarlet letter *I*. Living with a woman was bad enough; living with a woman who *knew* about him would be mortifying.

Ramming his fists inside his pockets, Ty scowled at the soft deck shoes he wore as slippers. "Look, if it's all the same to you, I'll pass on the dinner. It's getting pretty late—I've still got some reading to do."

"You're on a diet," Anny declared, ignoring his awkward excuses. "Don't be embarrassed, Ty. I go on periodic health kicks myself. Frankly, I think you're smart to take care of yourself, particularly now that you've retired from such an active occupation. What sort of exercise do you do?"

"What do you mean, exercise?"

"Pumping iron? Running?" She put away the sliced ham and took out an armload of vegetables and a carton of cottage cheese. "I've never seen you jogging around here. There are some great trails if you're interested."

Leaning back against the doorjamb again, Ty eased his guard slightly. "If you're waiting to see me get all dolled up in a fancy outfit and go puffing up and down your driveway, forget it. I don't mind walking—I'll even run if I have to, but I'll be damned if I'm going to make a production of it."

"Late starter, huh?" Anny shredded raw turnips and carrots over a bed of mixed greens. "How much exercise *have* you been getting since you retired?"

"How far would you say it is from F. G. Hall Laboratory to the parking lot? If it's raining, I walk moderately fast."

"That's *it*? No wonder you're so touchy. You should have started on a regular routine as soon as you stopped diving so that all that surplus energy wouldn't turn on you. I'll bet you're not sleeping too well either, are you?"

"What are you, some kind of a fitness freak?"

Busy with the salad she was concocting, Anny shook her head. "I just finished reading my way through Uncle Hannibal's health and nutrition books. He was sort of holistically inclined. I don't know if it had anything to do with his background in religious philosophy or not, but it makes sense to me.''

Ty hadn't the faintest idea what she was talking about, but he refused to hash over his most intimate problems with her—holistically, philosophically, or any other way.

''What's that stuff?'' Suspiciously, he eyed the yellowish powder she was dusting over the two enormous salads. He'd heard about some of these Oriental potency herbs, but he wasn't that desperate yet.

''Brewer's yeast. It's a great antidote for stress, full of lots of B vitamins and all that good stuff.''

''What the devil makes you think I need an antidote for stress?'' he demanded belligerently. Was that her snide way of telling him she'd guessed what his real problem was?

Shaking the oil and vinegar containers, Anny returned his look with one of growing amusement. The more cantankerous he grew, the more she warmed to him. Whether or not he admitted it, he needed her. No one had needed her since Hannibal, unless she counted all the owls she'd raised and the injured birds she'd nursed back to health.

''What does it taste like?'' Ty asked suspiciously.

''Brewer's yeast? With salad dressing, it's terrific. Any other way...'' She shrugged. ''What do you want to drink? Milk or buttermilk?''

Tyrus heaved a sigh of pure martyrdom. ''Milk.'' He watched while she poured. Then he put away the milk for her while she spread thick slices of brown bread with something from a stoneware crock, and he thought about the depths to which a man could sink in just a few short weeks.

In the living room, Anny raked the coffee table clear of assorted clutter and indicated his place. Settling herself onto the sofa, she took a long swallow of milk, licked the mustache from her upper lip, and turned to him with a look of determination. "Now...tell me about this health problem you're having."

Ty choked on a strip of raw turnip and grabbed his milk. When he'd caught his breath again, he returned her look with one of pure umbrage. "My health problems, Miss Cousins, are none of your damned business!"

Anny shrugged. Poking about in her salad for a raisin, she said, "No offense, but you do have a rotten disposition. You know, I think that's part of your trouble, Tyrus, and I have a few theories about it. Did you always?"

"Did I always what?" he demanded warily. Talking to Anny Cousins was about as safe as waltzing through a mine field.

"Have a rotten disposition. I'm almost sure it has something to do with not getting enough exercise. I used to be a real horror, too. I bit off heads for the sheer pleasure of spitting them out, but after I came to live with Uncle Hannibal, I got better. He kept bees and a diary, and he walked for miles every day, arthritis and all, just checking on things in general. Of course, it might have had something to do with the minerals in the water. No, that's kidney stones, isn't it?"

Ty gave up. He applied himself to his salad. So far, he'd identified nearly half the ingredients, and he didn't dare ask about the rest. It was filling, and not half bad once he got used to the textures.

"What do you do for entertainment, Tyrus?"

A few months ago he might have answered that he took Cass out to dinner every night, followed by a bit of dancing if he wasn't too bushed, and then they came back to the apartment, made love, and slept. About all he had in common with that uncle she'd mentioned was that he, too, had kept a diary of sorts, a log book in which he'd recorded some of the more interesting places he'd been and the dives he'd done.

There'd been no entries for over six months, and he didn't expect to be making any more. At this point his life was at its lowest ebb. He didn't know if the tide would ever turn again. "Entertainment?" he echoed bitterly. "I watch the leaves fall and make bets on which one will hit the ground first. Pretty heady stuff, huh?"

Hearing his own words, Ty winced. God, what a load of self-pitying bilge! This thing had cut even deeper than he'd realized. On his own since he was thirteen, he'd never been sick a day in his life. Whatever he was, whatever he had, he'd made it on his own, and until that day a few weeks ago when it had all crumbled into dust, he'd been extremely proud of what he'd accomplished.

Anny listened to the angry words, the bitter tone, and heard something more, something that touched a responsive chord deep inside her. A retired diver who looked to be in top condition, she mused. How on earth had he found his way to her doorstep? What was he doing here? What did he need from her?

A firm believer in fate, Anny leaned back, spread her arms along the back of the sofa, and smiled. She'd taken on an adult hawk only once. It hadn't worked out. She hadn't been physically strong enough.

She'd see if she could tame this one.

"There's always something going on at one or another of the colleges," she told him. "Do you like music? Theater? What about the zoo? There's a terrific zoo in Asheboro."

"Do I look like a kid to be taken to the zoo?"

Anny's gaze played over his powerful build, the deep, over-developed chest, the constriction of his hard hips, the blatant masculinity that clung to him like the clean, mossy scent of his soap. He probably hadn't looked like a kid since he was fourteen, but at the moment he certainly sounded like one. "Well, what *do* you enjoy?"

Rising, Ty began to prowl. "I enjoy women," he flung over his shoulder. "But not just any woman. I like my women to be beautiful and exciting. I like making love to them; I like watching them get dressed up to go out with me. I like watching them get undressed afterward." He stressed the latter, curling a malicious glance her way. "I like seeing them with their beautiful eyes all soft and glowing and their beautiful—" A smile twisted his mouth. "Shall I go on?"

Anny, her legs curled up beside her on the sofa, felt each word slice through the veneer she'd built up over the years to find a vulnerable target. There'd been other hurtful words in the past, words carelessly spoken by a man she'd fancied herself in love with, but none had cut quite so deeply, not since her fifteenth birthday. And this time it had been quite deliberate. Tyrus had meant to insult her, and for the life of her, she didn't know why. She'd only wanted to help.

To her disgust, she felt the prickling in her nose that indicated an onslaught of tears. Oh, damn! she swore silently. What *was* it with her crazy tear ducts? The major disasters of her life she'd met head on and dry-eyed, but just let something truly trivial happen to her, and she fell apart!

She fumbled through her pockets for a tissue and found only a paper towel wrapped around a broken arrowhead. Hannibal had had a theory; he'd compared the symptoms of colds with those of crying, claiming that if she hadn't regularly drained her system of its allotted tears, she'd have caught far more colds as a way of relieving her body of emotional stress. It had made her feel less of a fool. Besides, she hadn't had a cold since her early college days.

Ty, his shoulders hunched miserably, stood with his back to the room and stared at her reflection in the window. Dammit to hell! He'd hurt her feelings, and he honestly hadn't meant to. On the other hand, she'd been asking for it with all her prying and probing. Didn't the woman have sense enough to know that if he'd had any choice in the matter, he wouldn't even be here? He'd had to come up with something in a hurry, and this had sounded feasible. It wasn't working out, but that wasn't Anny's fault.

The plain truth was he was scared stiff. The medic in Wilmington had referred him to a physician in Durham, but he'd been afraid to go. What if he was worse? What if he'd be on those infernal pills forever, never able to make love to another woman?

As for entertainment, he could have gone out on the town. He'd had the chance. A couple of the E.M.I.'s who'd signed up for a clinical course on diving accidents had hit every nightspot in the area, and he could have gone along. One of the navy divers on loan for the upcoming deep-dive experiment had introduced him to several attractive women, but what the hell good was he to any woman? What if they'd come on to him?

The sound of a muffled hiccough reached through his preoccupation, and he turned. "Oh, hell, Anny..." He groaned, crossing to lower himself beside the huddled figure on the sofa.

"Don't you *dare* touch me," Anny warned. "I—I'm allergic."

"To all that health food, no doubt." The woman was bonkers. How could anyone who *talked* the way she did and *dressed* the way she did...and even *thought* the way she did have such a decided physical effect on him?

"At least I don't mope in my room when things don't go to suit me," she charged, rubbing her eyes and nose and then lifting a wet face to glare at him accusingly.

"I don't mope, as you call it." Red eyes, red nose, hair like a bird's nest, and she still looked good to him. His hands still itched to touch her. God, he was in worse shape than he'd thought.

Anny took a deep breath and faced the challenge she'd set for herself. If she backed down the first time he drew blood, she'd never be able to help him. It wasn't the first time she'd been injured. It probably wouldn't be the last. You cursed a little, cried a little, slapped on a disinfectant, and then got back to work.

"Go walking with me tomorrow," she challenged. "Get outdoors and pull some fresh air into your lungs and see if your manners won't improve. That was a cheap shot, and you know it. Looks aren't everything."

"It wasn't intentional, Anny." She smelled like soap. Not the exotic scented variety that Cass used, but the ordinary ninety-nine-and-forty-four-one-hundredths-percent-pure variety. He *must* be hard up if something like that could affect him this way.

"Yes, it was," she argued calmly, and Ty didn't bother to deny it again.

The truth was, she got under his skin, and it scared him. He'd meant to put her off by implying that she was neither beautiful nor interesting, but she was. In her own subtle, understated way, Anny was both. The trouble was, he couldn't handle a woman now—or possibly ever again. "You think walking will improve my disposition?"

"It can hardly make it worse," she retorted dryly, fully recovered from her momentary lapse. "You spend too much time sitting. First thing you know, you'll have a spare tire, and then you'll start having problems with cholesterol and blood pressure, and then your hair will go, and your eyes, and your feet will get flat, and your circulation will give you trouble."

"Is that all?" Flint-gray eyes permitted a shaft of amusement to break through.

"How are your teeth?"

"At least they're my own." He flashed her a grin, revealing a set of strong, white ones marred only by a single chip, and they both laughed.

It struck Anny that she'd never heard him laugh before. In fact, she could count the smiles he'd offered her on one hand. As he'd said that first day, Tyrus Clay was *not* a genial man. Nor a happy one, he'd added.

Feeling a warm strength flow into her body, she leaned back and regarded him thoughtfully. She didn't know the exact nature of his problem yet, but whatever it was, she'd definitely take him in hand. By the time he left her, he'd be a considerably happier, healthier person. After all, wasn't that her specialty? She was licenced by the state Wildlife Commission to rehabilitate raptors. A raptor, according to Webster, was a plunderer, a ravisher, a raptorial bird.

"Are you sure we're not lost?" Ty panted, collapsing against the trunk of a shagbark hickory tree.

"Trust me. I'm on a first-name basis with every tree in this corner of the county." Anny was tired, too, but not for the world would she admit it. The trouble was, they were both too proud, too stubborn. They'd walked some five or six miles, and neither would confess to wanting to turn back.

Ty's feet were killing him. With the start of the experimental dive still a week away, he'd been boning up on the first three simulated dives of the Atlantis series. When Anny had suggested an easy walk to get him started on an exercise schedule, he'd gone along with it. It hadn't occurred to him that he'd be this much out of shape already. Evidently, diving used a different set of muscles; an easy walk for Anny was a killer for him.

"Sure you wouldn't rather run?" he'd asked sarcastically after the first few hilly miles of rough terrain.

"You miss too much running. I'd rather walk fast and go farther."

The woman was incredible. She swung out in a long-legged stride, carrying a full load of gear on her back, yet she never seemed to tire.

Ty had plodded along all morning, the metal detector over his shoulder. The thing wasn't exactly light, either. He'd teased her about looking for treasure lost by some pirate who'd strayed too far up the Eno River, and she'd just smiled that maddening little smile of hers.

"Laugh all you want to. A smart pirate wouldn't think of burying his treasure along the seashore, where storms would wash it away. I get these flashes of intuition, and one of these days I'll home in on something besides rusty iron and pull tabs."

Anny indicated a clearing beside the river with conveniently placed rocks to serve as a picnic table. She was almost afraid to sit down for fear she wouldn't be able to get up again. And to think they still had to walk all those miles back! She wouldn't have done so much prancing around on all those little side trips if she'd known Ty was going to last this long—she'd gauged him for a couple of miles, at most. Divers weren't supposed to be terrific walkers, especially divers who didn't eat right and didn't exercise.

"Sprout sandwiches, farmer's cheese, and Jonathan apples. Here's yours."

"Oh, God, and for this I walked fifty miles?" Collapsing on a bed of leaves, Ty rubbed his knees and then began to massage his protesting calves. Who'd have guessed a man in the prime of life could go downhill so fast? "How many sandwiches did you make?"

It was almost dark by the time they got home. A red sunset reflected from flaming oaks, maples, and dogwoods to cast a flattering glow on the gaunt, white frame house. "I only have a shower downstairs," Anny observed, hooking the heels of her boots on the edge of the back porch and easing them off her sore feet.

"That's a real tragedy," Ty agreed.

"It's a small shower. You have to stand up in it."

"I'd say that was fair punishment for someone who stuffs a bale of hay between two slices of bread and calls it a square meal."

"I noticed you ate both of yours and one of mine, too." Divesting herself of camera and knapsack, Anny plucked her wool sweater away from her body. Walking was hot work.

"Tell you what I'll do. Go with me to the best seafood restaurant in town, and I'll let you soak in my bathtub." Ty's eyes gleamed their lazy, appreciative way down her rumpled body.

"You mean *now*? Like *this*?"

"Personally, I always strip to the buff first, but if you've got some hangup about peeling down for a bath…"

"I mean the restaurant. I don't think the place I have in mind would let me into the parking lot like this. I *itch*."

"I *starve*," Ty informed her. "Twenty minutes. You can spend them showering off or scratching. Suit yourself. Seafood's one thing I can eat my fill of, and tonight I've earned it."

Five minutes to shower, five to dry her hair, and ten to stare at the colorful dresses crammed into one end of her closet and wonder whether she could get by with corduroy slacks and a pullover.

Some totally unexpected element of vanity uncoiled like a genie from a bottle, and she reached for one of the things her mother had sent her from her father's last collection. Poor Claire, she never gave up hope of turning her grubby moth into a colorful butterfly.

At least the style was casual: a loose, cleverly cut top over a narrow skirt. The fabric made it. It was a heathery hand-loomed peach and plum. She'd worn it to dinner with Sid Chambers, her ex-fiancé and his family. Sid's wife, Janie, had asked if it had come from one of the nearby outlet stores. So much for haute couture.

At the last minute, she sprayed a whiff of the perfume Evan had sent for her birthday, and then she panicked and tried to rub it off again. Oh, beans! At this rate, she might as well stay home. Wholesome, earthy, practical Anny, in a tizzy just become some man had invited her out to dinner.

But then, when had she ever known a man like Tyrus? Certainly Sid had never brought about this fluttery feeling at the pit of her stomach. They'd been excellent friends, and that had been part of the trouble. That was *all* they'd been. No sparks, no excitement, none of this raw awareness she felt around Tyrus. She hadn't felt anything when he'd broken their engagement other than an obscure sense of relief that she wouldn't have to move into the ugly little brick bungalow he'd bought when he'd been made a full professor.

Ty was waiting for her in the living room. He turned to greet her, but the flip words he'd had ready died on his lips.

This was Anny? This tall, lovely creature in pink was the woman who froze mice and crawled in attics and dressed like a lumberjack every day to go tramping through the woods?

"Don't look at me," Anny muttered stiffly. "I embarrass easily."

"What's to be embarrassed about?"

"I don't know," she retorted, "but I am, and if you laugh, I'll brain you." For someone conditioned from birth to a man's scrutiny of every scrap of clothing she wore, she wasn't doing too well. "Don't take it personally. I think I must be coming down with a case of delayed adolescence."

Ty helped her on with a lightweight coat, his hands lingering at her shoulders until she ducked away. "You look lovely, Anny."

"Well, frankly, you do, too." She grinned as her momentary embarrassment faded and a very real appreciation took its place. In flannels, a tweed jacket, and a dark wool shirt, he was enough to make her forget the role she'd set out to play in his life.

They took his car, and Anny gave clear, concise directions. She wondered if he was as tired as she was. Her feet, in the unaccustomed high-heeled pumps, were killing her. It was her own fault. If she hadn't been so determined not to be the first one to give in, they wouldn't have hiked so far over rugged, rocky terrain. Looking back, she had to admit that she'd set a brisker pace and done a lot more rock-hopping than she normally did.

Food would help. And wine. A long soak in a tub filled with hot water would have been heavenly; barring that, about three glasses of chilled white wine should take away most of the pain.

The parking lot was crowded, and Anny congratulated herself on having secured last-minute reservations. Once seated, she smiled tentatively and looked around the room before slipping off her shoes under the table. This was her parents' favorite restaurant, perhaps because it sat on what had once been LeMontrose property, and Claire was always given the royal treatment.

As a flock of penguinlike attendants descended on them, it occurred to Anny that it was about time for another parental visitation. She groaned inwardly.

"Would you like a drink, or would you rather go directly to the main event?" Ty asked.

"A drink, please."

"Something organic and healthful, I suppose. Buttermilk?"

"That does it. I was going to order a glass of the house white, but just for that, I think I'll have the most expensive thing on the wine list."

"That'll show me, huh?" Grinning, he conferred briefly with the wine steward and settled on a Pouilly-Fuissé.

A male vocalist provided a nostalgic menu of fifties music, and when two couples got up to dance, Ty leaned across the table, twin devils lurking in his eyes. "I understand dancing is considered pretty good exercise. Would you care to go a few rounds with me?"

"Only if you can guarantee that my feet won't touch the floor."

"Maybe we'd better hold off until the blisters go down."

By the time they'd demolished a tray of crab, lobster, oysters, and shrimp, and a matched pair of perfectly broiled swordfish steaks, the wine bottle was empty. Anny could have curled up in a corner and slept quite happily. Her feet no longer hurt. Nothing hurt. Over dinner, Tyrus had regaled her with several highly improbable tales of sunken treasure and the men who hunted it, and she'd countered with a few stories of her own: one concerning a hand-raised great-horned owl that terrorized every outdoor dinner party in the neighborhood by landing in the middle of the table and helping himself, and another about a badly trained falcon that began diving on gray-haired men, evidently mistaking them for wild rabbits.

Gradually, the well-dressed patrons began to depart and the bustle of tuxedoed waiters receded, leaving a warm oasis of candlelit silver and sparkling wineglasses. Anny allowed her imagination to run unchecked for a little while, wondering what it would be like to lie in those capable arms, to bury her hands in that sooty hair, to taste those firm, sensuous lips.

Tyrus, sated with salty raw oysters, succulent swordfish, and the crisp, dry wine, dragged himself free of a pair of lambent eyes. God, it had been all he could do not to lick the melted butter from her lips. How could any woman so candid, so completely guileless, get to him this way? "I'd better get you home while I can still move under my own steam," he murmured gruffly, moving around the table to stand behind her. His hands brushed her hair, hair the color of Sargasso weed, the texture of spun silk, and he held her chair.

"I think I've lost something," Anny murmured.

"Shall I call the waiter?"

"See if they're over on your side of the table, will you?" She was whispering, and as the music started up again, Ty leaned over to catch her words and inhaled the soft fragrance of her perfume. His hand moved from the chair to her shoulders, and he felt the delicacy of her bones through the soft-rough fabric of her dress. "Give me a clue. Your purse? Your napkin?"

"My shoes," she whispered. The heat of his body encircled her, wrapping her in the aura of his subtle after-shave. Unconsciously, she leaned into the circle of his embracing arm.

Reluctantly, Ty allowed his arm to slide away. He knelt and folded back the table cover, retrieving her shoes from underneath. Anny drew in a sharp breath as he lifted one foot and eased the cool leather over her toes, his palm warming her ankle as he slid the strap over her heel. By the time he'd replaced both of the open-toed, sling-backed pumps, she was entertaining visions of tattered nylons, melted by the touch of his incendiary fingers.

Breathing heavily, Ty stood, drawing her up with him. He dropped a large bill on the table and led her out to the foyer. As he held her coat while she slid her arms into the sleeves, he fought down the gnawing insistence of still another hunger, one that had gone unsatisfied for far too long.

Five

—————

 Let's get out of here," Ty growled abruptly, putting her away from him and striding off toward the car. The small parking lot had been filled when they'd arrived, and they'd had to park in an unpaved annex.

Anny's lips tightened as she watched him stride away. So much for her good intentions; she should have known that a feral animal could never be completely trusted.

"Don't let me keep you," she muttered, ruining her delicate suede heels as she hurried after him.

Ty halted in his tracks, turning to retrace the few steps between them. "Oh, hell, Anny, I'm sorry."

"No problem, I can keep up with you."

"On land, maybe," he conceded, taking her arm as they neared his car.

"You intended to swim home?" She yanked it free and reached for the door. It was locked, of course. Feeling both gauche and dangerously vulnerable, she allowed him to help her into the low bucket seat. As idiotic as it was, the man had only to touch her and she melted.

There were certain drawbacks to living a solitary life, Anny mused as they left Durham behind, one of the more important being the loss of a woman's natural immunity to an attractive man.

The ride home took some thirty-five minutes. Anny was thankful for the brusque patter of the newscaster Ty tuned in on the radio. Hearing a rundown of the latest local and national crises put her own emotional problems into proper perspective. By the time they pulled up under the red oak tree, she'd managed once more to explain away her irrational reaction to the man fate had temporarily dumped on her doorstep.

Nothing had really happened. Absolutely nothing. They'd walked too far, come home tired and hungry, gone out together and shared a meal and a bottle of wine. Naturally, they'd talked and laughed over dinner. Naturally, she'd dropped her guard as she grew more relaxed in his company; under the circumstances, it was only to be expected.

Then he'd happened to touch her in the course of helping her on with her coat and her shoes, and because she'd been tired, because the wine had affected her metabolism or her judgment, she'd overreacted. That's all it was, all it could be. Ty was an attractive man, and she was a normal, healthy woman.

Instead of going around to his private entrance, Ty joined her as she was digging about in her purse for her keys. He took them from her hand, unlocked the front door, and followed her inside. Neither of them had spoken a single word since leaving the restaurant, and Anny, her tongue cleaving to the roof of her mouth, searched for the words that would end the evening on just the right note.

"Well?" Ty challenged, thumbs hooked under his belt.

Anny could picture him on the deck of a ship, his eyes a perfect match for the stormy skies as he braced against mountainous seas. "Well, what?"

"Well, what are you sulking about?"

"*Sulking* about!" she exploded. "You stalk off across the parking lot and leave me to find my own way, you bite my head off for no reason at all, and then you accuse me of *sulking*?"

"Forty-five minutes without a single word? What else would you call it?" He had yet to meet a woman who didn't try sulking to get her way. Cass had it down to a fine art. On the other hand, it was hardly fair to compare two women who weren't even in the same league.

"*Thirty*-five minutes, and I was listening to the news."

"Forty. I timed it. I didn't realize you were such an avid sports fan." The news had been followed by an interminable rehash of the day's games.

"You seemed so enthralled, I hated to interrupt," Anny countered, actually beginning to enjoy the match as she detected a gleam of lazy amusement behind those stern features.

Tyrus moved a step closer, drawn by a tiny quiver of laughter that trembled at the corners of her mouth. Toe to toe, eye to eye, they confronted one another, each daring the other to break. It was a crazy confrontation about nothing in particular, and yet Anny felt the adrenaline race through her body, leaving nerves taut, senses heightened to an incredible degree. Flint-colored eyes bored into acorn-brown ones, searching for a hint of weakness; silver glinted against the ebony of his hair, and against all reason, Anny's fingers burned to smooth the unruly strands back from his high forehead.

"Still not talking?" Ty drawled.

Trying for a look of disdain, Anny shrugged. If a battle of wills was what he wanted, then she was more than ready to accommodate him. For reasons that eluded her at the moment, though, it was important that she win.

"There are ways to loosen that tongue of yours," Ty suggested softly. "And you're determined to force me to demonstrate, aren't you?"

The velvet gauntlet lay between them, surrounded by an aura of vibrant tension. Anny, with a recklessness heretofore unknown, threw back her head and raised her brows disdainfully. If the house had suddenly burst into flames, she could not have moved from the spot.

The harsh rasp of Ty's breath ripped through her consciousness an instant before he reached for her. There was no time to escape. Long afterward, Anny saw herself as if in a slow-motion film, swaying toward him, lips parting just as his fingers captured her jaw.

Holding her captive with work-roughened hands, his eyes gone strangely dark, Ty brushed his lips against hers, slowly, lingeringly, as though intent on exploring the texture of her mouth. The vital force of his potent magnetism wrapped around her, seeping in to undermine what little strength she possessed. And still he didn't crush her to him as she longed to be crushed.

Anny stifled a small moan as his baffling restraint continued to frustrate her efforts to move closer. Helplessly, she bared the long line of her throat to his predatory attentions.

"Ivory," Ty whispered against the vulnerable underside of her chin. "Warm, living ivory."

She felt the hot moistness of his kisses along the side of her throat and sagged against him. With her face held between his hands, his powerful forearms prevented her from moving any closer, and she twisted, trying vainly to slip inside the barrier. *Hold me, hold me, damn you!* she cried silently. *Don't do this to me!* What was wrong with the man? What was wrong with her?

Ty kissed each corner of her lips and then traced the line between them with the tip of his tongue, and Anny moaned softly, ignoring the voice of pride that bade her to walk away. He was doing it deliberately, she decided as, distraught, she ran her fingers up his arms and pried gently at the tender barricade of his hands.

"You taste like lily of the valley," he murmured in her ear.

"My perfume..."

"And you smell like apricot brandy."

"My dessert." Anny caught at his lip with her teeth, barely resisting the urge to bite down hard. She was furious with him. She was starving for him, and he insisted on driving her wild by merely nibbling around the edges.

"So now I'll have my dessert," Tyrus rasped as his hands slid around her finally to draw her tightly against him.

There was nothing restrained in the hard male body that bruised her softness, nor in the hungry mouth that plundered her willing lips. His hands roamed restlessly up and down her back, and Anny felt the bones in her legs begin to liquefy. The incoherent sounds that emerged from her throat were like nothing she'd ever heard before—and certainly like nothing she'd ever uttered.

The taste of him was wildly intoxicating, driving out all semblance of reason. Her breasts longed for his touch, and when she felt the flat of his palm slide up from her hips to move around her rib cage, she shifted to accommodate him, feeling the firm crests tighten thrillingly in anticipation of his touch.

Suddenly, so suddenly that she nearly lost her balance, Ty thrust her from him and turned away. Against the soft sounds of an old house settling in for the night, his breath tore out, harsh and ragged.

The back of her hand pressed against lips that were still throbbing, Anny leaned against the wall. Slowly, painfully, the bittersweet tide subsided. *God, won't I ever learn?* Anger flowed in to fill the void as passion seeped away, and she forced herself to breathe deeply. *Count to ten*, she ordered silently; *don't say one word until you count to ten*.

She got as far as seven, and then Ty turned to regard her with the same forbidding look she'd come to expect from him during the early days. It was a look that said, "Don't tread on me."

In the end, it was his very outrageousness that tipped the scales in his favor. The wilder the hawk, Anny reminded herself, the more frightened he'd be. And this hawk needed her. Either he was going through a period of self-doubt brought on by his early retirement, or he was having woman trouble. The first she could help him with, but she refused to allow herself to be used as a stand-in for some other woman.

"If you'd like to walk again tomorrow," she said with commendable composure, "I'll be ready when you get home."

Cool slate eyes turned evasive, shifted away, and Ty muttered something about working late.

She shrugged. "The next day, then. Don't let it drop after such a great beginning." She refused to let him sink back into the well of apathy he'd been wallowing in before.

"Don't you think this charade has gone far enough, little Miss Do-Good?"

Anny smiled, her confidence returning in illogical proportion to Ty's surliness. "You want to turn into a heap of flab? You want to hole up in a cubbyhole on campus all day and then come home and hide out in your room?" Turning toward her bedroom, she collected the coat that had slithered unheeded to the floor. "Go ahead, then. Whoever she is, you must be pretty confident that she'll want you regardless of what shape you're in. Must be your charming personality you're counting on."

"Knock it off, Anny."

Bemused, Anny watched as he strode across the room and took the crooked, sloping stairs two at a time. Any man who could do that without coming to grief couldn't be in such bad shape, she mused.

So there was a woman. Sighing, she removed her dress and tossed it over a chair, then slipped off her shoes and stood before a mirror clad only in a slip and nylons. "What did you expect, fool?" she asked the clouded image.

Objectively, she examined what she saw, found it wanting, but not distressingly so. She peeled the straps of her slip from her shoulders and let it slither down her body to the floor. What *had* she expected, for pity's sake? That Prince Charming would trot up her graveled road on a dusty white charger, toss her across his saddle and gallop off to his castle?

Fat chance. What did they say about tens attracting tens and twos attracting twos? It made sense. On any woman's scale, Ty was a resounding ten. Sid had probably rated a solid six. If she hadn't even been able to hold on to a six, what did that make her?

"Dismal," she uttered with a wry grin. "Pretty dismal. Now I know why I always hated math."

Tyrus awoke to the sound of someone chopping wood under his window. It brought into fleeting focus a memory, the jagged edges of which had long since lost their ability to wound. Under a white-hot August sky, an overgrown kid with a newly broken nose had split mountains of cord wood and stacked it to dry. Hands soft from years of boardinghouse dishwashing had blistered quickly, and the blisters had broken, sticking to the shiny hickory wood of the axe handle.

The pain had been agonizing. He'd cursed with precocious ease and chopped all the harder. As soon as he'd earned enough, he was getting out of town. With his mother gone and the old waterfront boardinghouse where he'd grown up bulldozed to make way for a warehouse, there was no longer anything to hold him back.

One thing he'd known for sure; no S.O.B. would ever call him names again and get away with it. He'd been born in that damned boardinghouse, and he'd worked there before and after school, more to help his mother than for any other reason. She'd worn herself out in the big, inconvenient kitchen, too proud to accept help from any of the merchant seamen who patronized the place.

Ty had many memories of awakening in the night as he was being carried from his mother's room. He'd always been bedded down in the laundry room next door on a pile of sheets that smelled of lye soap. He hadn't really minded; the sheets were a hell of a lot softer than his cot, and those were the only times his mother ever laughed. And if the muffled giggles that came through the thin partition happened to be mingled with deeper, rougher laughter, so what? Any laughter was better than none at all.

Hell, he might have been fathered in that very room. He'd been named for two honorary uncles who were regular boarders when he was still in short pants. Tyler Cornatzer and Russell Fortis, both merchant seamen who'd taken a passing interest in Cora May's boy whenever they were in port. Both men had families back east, and they'd stopped coming around altogether a few years before Cora had died.

Ty had lied his way out from under the authorities, hustled whatever jobs were available until he'd saved enough for a stake, and then he'd headed for Galveston, where he'd found himself a berth on a trawler. The first year, he'd earned his keep and little more, but he'd taken to the water and he'd learned fast. If diving hadn't sidetracked him, he'd have earned himself a master's ticket by now.

A chunk of wood hit the side of the house, and Anny's voice came clearly through the closed windows.

"Beans! Will you *stop* falling over before I even *hit* you?"

Dragging the bedspread with him, Ty crossed to throw open the window. After lying awake half the night, he was in no mood to be awakened at the crack of dawn, especially as he didn't have to be at the lab until after lunch.

"Hey, how about taking your beans and your wood-pile around to the other side of the house?"

Leaning on her axe handle, Anny shielded her eyes against the sun. "Aren't you up yet?"

"Obviously."

"No need to be sarcastic. How was I to know you were planning to sleep all day? What's the matter? Did I wear you out yesterday?" An insouciant grin accompanied the words, and Tyrus slammed down the window.

"You wore me out, all right, you freckle-faced witch," he grumbled, heading for the bathroom. He'd had the devil's own time getting to sleep, and then his dreams had been plagued by visions he'd be better off without. "Damn women, anyway," he muttered, grimacing at the bearded image in the mirror. "Tantalize a man, lead him on, and..."

"Apricot-pecan muffins," Anny called out half an hour later. Ty, dressed in the soft corduroys and one of the flannel shirts he favored, was reaching for his attaché case with the idea of going to the university early and finding a quiet corner of the library.

"I'm not hungry. Thanks," he added grudgingly.

"Sure you are. You're just too big a coward to admit it."

Anny glanced up as her kitchen door was blocked by a solid mass of angry male. "What the hell is that supposed to mean?" Ty snarled.

She continued to split the steaming nuggets, spreading them with a creamy cottage cheese mixture. "Look, if you want to crawl into your shell and feel sorry for yourself just because you're too old to dive any longer, feel free. It's no skin off my nose.''

Ty slung his attaché case across the table and glared at her. "I do *not* feel sorry for myself! And I'm not too old to dive!"

"Whatever you say, Flipper. I located another floor-lamp for you. I'll get it up to your room today and lay in a supply of hundred-fifty-watt bulbs. I read somewhere that the older a person is, the more light they requi—"

"There's nothing wrong with my eyes!"

"Don't be embarrassed about it. We all get old—if we're lucky."

"I am *not* getting old, dammit!" Ty seethed.

Anny glanced up, a tranquil smile on her lips and a look of highly suspect innocence in her deep amber eyes. "You're not? Is that what you've been working on in the lab—a formula for perpetual youth? Hmm, might have commercial possibilities, but did you ever stop to think of the social impact?"

"Anny." The warning was a low, guttural sound at the back of his throat as Tyrus moved a threatening step closer.

She held out a muffin and Ty ignored it, glowering at her across the small table. "Oh, come on, now, can't you take a joke? I was just trying to perk up your circulation."

"Leave my circulation out of this." His eyes bored into hers, and Anny dropped the muffin to the table. It rolled onto the floor.

"Oh, well—I guess if you're going to stay young forever, you don't have to worry about that sort of thing, do you?" A small pulse trembled at the side of his throat, and Anny resisted the urge to touch it.

"The only thing I have to worry about," Ty said between clenched teeth, "is *high blood pressure*! And you're not doing one damned thing to help!" His hands came down on her shoulders, fingers like steel talons biting into her bones.

"Tyrus, I'm so sorry. I had no idea," Anny cried. Covering his hands with her cottage-cheesey ones, she added "Why didn't you just tell me to mind my own business?"

A wintry smile came and went on Ty's lean visage, and he dropped his hands. "Now, why didn't that occur to me, I wonder?"

"You did, didn't you?" Anny asked meekly. "I'm a meddling fool. No wonder you didn't want to—but Tyrus, why didn't you tell me?" she rushed on earnestly. "Ty, you know we were on the right track all along—exercise works wonders. How high is it? How long have you known? Is that why you had to give up diving?"

"In reverse order, yes, and a couple of months, and not dangerously, and so I was told."

Anny's mouth dropped open as she fumbled to slot the answers into the proper questions. Before she'd quite succeeded, Ty picked up one of her freshly baked muffins and shoved it between her teeth. Collecting his briefcase, he let himself out the back door, tossing a look over his shoulder that came back more than once to puzzle her as she worked in her studio that day.

It was a day of interruptions. First there were the hunters wanting permission to use the land along the river. Anny referred them to the owner, who had a strictly enforced no-hunting policy. Susan Macklin called to see if the illustrations could be finished within a month.

"What about the last batch—the winter ones? I'd planned on a snow scene to show the tracks of various animals that use the river as a thoroughfare."

"Could you fake it?"

"I'd rather not. What's the rush? I thought I had at least until February."

"Would you like lead-title status on our modest spring list? Would you like to be showcased at the next A.B.A.? I just found out that O'Hara's nature-walk series is being reissued in a boxed set for Christmas, and if we can get the new one out this spring while it's still fresh, we'll have it made."

"Glory be," Anny murmured, absently picking up a pencil line with a wad of kneaded eraser. O'Hara had been out of print for almost fifteen years. For at least ten of those he'd been nagging his New York publisher to reissue his old titles. In disgust, he'd finally given up, and practically in his dotage, he'd signed with Persimmon Press to do one more book.

"Just pray for early snow," Susan said. "Meanwhile, do the best you can, and we'll work around you."

The phone rang again before Anny had even uncapped her drawing pen. This time it was Claire calling to say she and Evan would be coming through on their way to New York.

"Book us our usual, darling. And why don't you plan to spend a few days at the hotel with us? I have to see Papa's lawyer while I'm here, so it will take an extra day or so."

"Mother, I'm in the middle of an assignment, and I'm pushing a deadline."

"A few days with your father and mother? Sweetheart, is that too much to ask?"

Anny shoved ink-stained fingers through her untidy hair and grimaced. "It's not just that," she prevaricated. "I—uh—have someone staying here now."

"More of those disgusting creatures, I suppose," Claire snapped. "Well, if a shoebox full of naked birds means more to you than—"

"It's a man." Despairingly, Anny waited out the pregnant silence that followed. She'd never found the nerve to confess to renting out her spare room; her father would have found a way to put an end to it, one way or another. As it was, they tolerated her eccentricities by putting them down to artistic temperament.

"A man?"

"Yes, a man. You can meet him if you like, but I don't need your approval, Mother. I'm thirty-four years old, remember?"

"I'd just as soon forget." Claire's shudder was almost audible. "All right, darling, I'll try to prepare your father, but don't blame me if he has a fit. You're still his little girl, even if you are old enough to go your own stubborn way."

Thoroughly depressed, Anny went back to work. She'd never been Evan's "little girl"...not in that sense. Evan hadn't particularly cared for children. He'd confessed the shortcoming frequently, as though it were a minor and somehow endearing trait. As an adult, Anny had tried to forgive and forget. She'd managed to forgive, but she could never forget the feelings of inadequacy that had followed her through the years.

The next time the phone rang, she slammed down her pen and lunged for it, practically screeching a greeting into the receiver.

See over the page for details

![D] Silhouette Desire

ANNOUNCING SILHOUETTE READER SERVICE

ARIEL BERK
Promise Of Love

SUZANNE MICHELLE
Sweetheart Of A Deal

ANN MAJOR
The Wrong Man

ERIN ROSS
Odds Against

Experience all the excitement, passion and pure joy of love. Send for your **FOUR FREE** Silhouette Desire novels today.

Postage will be paid by Licensee

Do not affix postage stamps if posted in Gt. Britain, Channel Islands or N. Ireland.

BUSINESS REPLY SERVICE
Licence No. CN 81

Silhouette Reader Service,
PO Box 236, Thornton Road,
CROYDON, Surrey CR9 9EL.

2

Silhouette Desire are love stories that go *beyond* other romances — taking you behind closed doors, to share the intense, intimate moments between a man and a woman united by love.

These are fascinating stories of successful modern women, who are in charge of their lives and career — and in charge of their hearts. Confident women who face the challenge of today's world and its obstacles to attain their dreams and their desires.

At last an opportunity for you to become a regular reader of Silhouette Desire. You can enjoy 6 superb new titles every month from Silhouette Reader Service with a whole range of special benefits: a free monthly Newsletter packed with recipes, competitions, exclusive book offers and a monthly guide to the stars, plus extra bargain offers and big cash savings.

As a special introduction we will send you Four specially selected Silhouette Desire Romances when you complete and return this card.

At the same time, because we believe that you will be so thrilled with these novels we will reserve a subscription to Silhouette Reader Service for you. Every month you will receive 6 of the very latest novels by leading Romantic Fiction authors, delivered direct to your door. And they cost the same as they would in the shops — postage and packing is always completely Free. There is no obligation or commitment — you can cancel your subscription at any time.

It's so easy. Send no money now — you don't even need a stamp. Just fill in and detach this card and send it off today.

FREE BOOKS CERTIFICATE

NO STAMP NEEDED

To: Silhouette Reader Service, FREEPOST,
   PO Box 236, Thornton Road, Croydon, Surrey CR9 9EL

Please send me, Free and without obligation, four specially selected Silhouette Desire Romances and reserve a Reader Service Subscription for me. If I decide to subscribe, I shall, from the beginning of the month following my free parcel of books, receive six books each month for £5.94, post and packing free. If I decide not to subscribe I shall write to you within 10 days. The free books are mine to keep in any case. I understand that I may cancel my subscription at any time simply by writing to you. I am over 18 years of age. *Please write in BLOCK CAPITALS.*

Name_____ Signature_____

Address_____

_____ Postcode_____

SEND NO MONEY — TAKE NO RISKS
Remember postcodes speed delivery. Offer applies in U.K. only and is not valid to present subscribers, overseas send for details. Silhouette reserve the right to exercise discretion in granting membership. If price changes are necessary you will be notified. Offer expires 30th June 1986.

2S6SD

"I beg your pardon," came the hesitant contralto response. "I must have the wrong number. I was trying to reach Tyrus Clay."

Anny heaved a long-suffering sigh. "Sorry—the phone company can't seem to get that awful squawk out of my line," she lied unabashedly. "This is Ty's number—I mean, he lives here, but he's not here at the moment. Could I have him call you?"

"Who are you?" the caller asked pointblank.

Rudeness begat rudeness. Anny considered retracting her impulsive lie. "I'm Anny Cousins, Miss—"

"Valenti. You live there, too?"

"Yes."

Once more she was subjected to a lengthy silence, during which her imagination shifted into overdrive. She'd always gotten along well with women, but somehow she had a feeling that this woman might prove to be an exception.

"Look, just tell Ty that Cass called, will you? I'll be in Raleigh on business next week. I'll give him a ring when I find out exactly when and where I'll be staying."

Anny sat for several minutes with her hand on the phone. Cass Valenti. Could this be the woman in Ty's life?

"So the man's spoken for. He can always use another friend, can't he?" she reasoned aloud. Why spoil her record of remaining friends with old lovers?

Pity they couldn't have been lovers first, though.

She switched off her work light and went down to the kitchen, where she conscientiously devoured the rest of the muffins and started in on a half-empty carton of chocolate ice cream.

Six

Without ever making an issue of it, Anny persuaded Ty to continue exercising on a regular basis. She didn't pretend to be an expert on health, but if disposition was anything to go by, his was greatly improved by an hour or so of splitting firewood, or a brisk few miles of walking through the wooded trails each day.

After long hours bent over a drawing board, she needed the exercise even more than Ty did. She put in additional hours in the studio each night now that she was no longer intimidated by his presence in the room next door. If her concentration wasn't all it should be, that couldn't be helped. It was her problem; she'd deal with it the best way she could.

With no conscious decision on Anny's part, the metal detector stayed home. Excitement no longer seemed dependent on the chance discovery of an esoteric scrap of metal. The field drawings finished, she left her camera and knapsack behind, as well.

On a day when a cold, damp wind stripped gold and scarlet leaves from the trees to hurl them about like confetti, Anny threw back her head and filled her lungs deeply, alive with a sense of well-being. It was almost time to turn back, and they'd been gone little more than an hour. By the time Ty got home each day, the autumn sun was already casting long, blue shadows.

They paused to watch a whitetail buck munching on acorns before turning back. Halfway home, at a curve in the river Anny had nicknamed The Stockade because of the many pointed tree stumps on both banks, they glimpsed the beaver responsible for the elaborate reconstruction project.

A few yards ahead, Ty halted suddenly, extending a hand for silence. Anny allowed herself a brief survey of his lean, powerful build, her gaze sweeping downward from a set of shoulders that threatened the seams of his navy wool shirt and lingering on the narrowed shape of his hips before moving down those long swimmer's legs. For a moment, her imagination took off and soared like one of the colorful leaves that swirled overhead before coming to rest on the carpeted forest floor. *He'd be something to see in a wetsuit.* She noted with a tender smile that his feet were planted in the stance she'd come to think of as his on-deck position. Tyrus against the world.

"What is it?" she whispered belatedly, resisting the impulse to take the extended hand.

"You tell me. I heard it twice. Sounds like something from a Tarzan film." It came again, a plaintive, broken cry. "There!" Ty whispered tersely. "What the devil *is* it?" He continued to listen, head tilted at an angle, eyes narrowed. "It sounds either tropical or...prehistoric."

Anny's lips trembled. Her eyes brimmed over with laughter, and she bent to rest her bottom on the trunk of an oak, bracing her hands on her knees.

A wisp of sound escaped her, and Ty pivoted silently. "Anny?"

Helplessly, she shook her head, and then the laughter bubbled forth like an artesian spring.

"Anny?" He moved a threatening step closer, and she slid to the ground and buried her face in her hands, shoulders shaking.

"What the hell—! Anny, are you laughing or crying? I'll be damned if I can figure you out, woman."

A hand closed over the back of her neck, and she struggled to get herself under control. It wasn't all that funny, actually. "It's a crow, Ty. A common old crow." She collapsed again at his expression of outraged disbelief. "Honestly, it—it is, Ty. They're such mimics. This one's obviously a Tarzan fan, too."

"Are you making fun of me?" he demanded, and Anny howled all the harder. She'd always expressed her surface emotions too easily; laughter and tears came readily enough. It was only the deeper feelings that got all tangled up inside her until they felt like a dry, hard pain in her chest.

Wrestling her to the ground, Ty followed her down, dragging her hands away to scowl down at her. Gradually, the scowl gave way to a look of wariness, not untouched by concern.

Hovering helplessly between giggles and tears, Anny bit her trembling lower lip as she met his eyes unflinchingly. Lord, what was happening to her? Her emotions were all over the road these days!

"Anny..." The word was a sigh that cooled her flushed face a moment before his mouth came down on hers.

The world slipped from her grasp and spun out of control as Anny felt herself pressed into the cold, damp bed of leaves. Her arms crept up to draw her burden even closer, and she knew a moment's fierce resentment at the barriers of flannel and corduroy, wool and suede.

Feverishly, her palms stroked his back, memorizing the contours of the taut muscles that sprang from the deep valley of his spine. He tasted of apples gone winey. As his kisses grew more invasive, the rasp of his late-day beard scraped against her skin, exciting a rush of goose bumps along her flanks.

His hands sought her breasts, struggled with the zipper of her jacket, and then collided with her own fingers as she sought to unbutton both shirts. Her fingertips raked across a bed of wiry hair and tangled frustratingly in the folds of his shirt. Before she could free them, she felt his calloused touch on her naked flesh. Instantly, nerve endings fused together in an insistent clamor as heat invaded the core of her being. She strained in a desperate need to press herself closer.

"Ah-hhh, Anny, don't do this to me," Ty grated just before his mouth possessed the soft mounds his hands had already claimed. For one fleeting moment, she had the craziest impression, as if he were drawing her closer and pushing her away at the same time.

When his lips closed over the throbbing button that thrust between his fingers, Anny gasped aloud. With shaking hands, she reached up to hold his head between her hands, loving the feel of his soft-crisp hair, his long, flat ears, his lean, deeply tanned cheeks. Loving...

"Anny, Anny, what are you doing to me?"

The rough whisper caressed her vulnerable flesh, burning away the chill of the encroaching shadows, as he began to forge a pathway of kisses down the opened front of her shirt. His hands fumbled at the waistband of her jeans, and her fingers moved convulsively in their desire to open the way for him.

Shifting his position, Ty let his full weight rest on the length of her body for one long moment. Then, with a groan dredged up from the very depths of his soul, he rolled away and sat up, his back to her.

Beyond dissimulation, Anny could only stare at him, a mixture of desire and disappointment clouding her gaze. Didn't he want her, after all? Had all the wanting been on her part?

No, he'd wanted her, all right. She might not be the most experienced woman in the world, but even *she* knew that much!

After brushing the leaves from her hair, she pulled down her chemise and rebuttoned her shirt, sending frequent puzzled glances to the broad back Ty had turned her way. He was staring off into the shadowy trees, his breathing, she noted with annoyance, perfectly under control. Damned swimmer!

Not until her own breathing had returned to normal did she venture a few brittle words. "Was it something I said?"

"What?" Twisting around, Ty raked a crooked path through his hair with his fingers. "Oh, hell, Anny, I'm too old to go rolling around on the hard ground in the middle of winter."

She forced him to meet her eyes, forced herself to ignore the rise of heat that stained her cheeks. "Winter? You *are* a hothouse flower, aren't you? Seems to me I'm the one who should be complaining; at least you had a warm, dry mattress."

Ty's smile was strained, but she gave him credit for the attempt. "Sort of lumpy in spots, now that you mention it."

She wanted to be angry with him—*needed* to be angry with him—but she simply couldn't. "Insult my lumps at your own peril. For that you're going to find your own way home." Rising with a ballet-like grace, she spun away before he could get to his feet.

"Anny!" he bellowed after her. "Anny, come back here!" The words echoed in the dusky stillness as she dodged between the trees and cut across the path on a direct route home.

Anny tackled her conscience the minute she arrived in her warm, untidy kitchen. The man deserved a little discomfort for leading her on and then dropping her flat.

But there was Cass, she reminded herself. She'd known about Cass and still she'd let herself dream. If he took what she offered and walked away, could she blame anyone but herself?

Oh, Lord, he was probably thoroughly lost by now, stumbling along the riverbed, wet to the skin, freezing...

Any man who could find his way around the bottom of the ocean without the benefit of a map could certainly follow a path through the woods, even in the fading light. Besides, he needed to learn his way around. If she got in a bind on those drawings, he'd have to walk alone if he walked at all.

By the time Ty made it back home, Anny had fought her conscience to a standstill. She was heating the meat-less black bean soup she'd made the day before, when he emerged from the woods. Relief a palpable feeling in-side her, she watched his progress from the edge of the second-growth pines, past the empty mews, past the stands where Hannibal's bee boxes once had stood. He paused to lean against the stack of firewood they'd both contributed to before tackling the last few yards to the back porch. He was limping.

Wiping her hands on her corduroy jeans, she stepped through the door. "Ty, are you all right?"

"Do I look all right?"

He looked more than all right. He looked beautiful. "You're limping."

"All sympathy, aren't you? Heartless wench. You didn't even leave me a trail of breadcrumbs to follow."

Tension drained away—tension she wasn't even aware of having harbored. "Birds would have eaten them. We've got a strain of prehistoric crows around these parts that are real bread crumb connoisseurs. What hap-pened? Did you twist your ankle?"

"Would you care?" He shot her a baleful look, sat on the edge of the porch, and slipped the soft-soled deck shoe from his foot to massage his heel.

Riddled with fresh guilt, Anny squatted beside him and reached for his foot. He stood, one shoe off, one on, and glared down at her. "What do you want to do, break the other one?"

"I shouldn't have let you walk in those shoes," she murmured.

"If you think I'm going to get myself dressed up in fancy racing gear, you're crazy. These shoes have taken me from the Pacific to the Gulf Coast to the Atlantic. They ought to be good for a few miles along the Eno.''

Anny swallowed the smile that trembled as she let him in the back door. Instead of a head-on confrontation, she decided on the oblique approach. ''I'm heating supper. Why not go soak the aches and pains out and then come on down for a bowl of black bean soup?''

''Thanks, but I've got some paperwork to catch up on.''

''Floorlamp working out okay?'' She lifted the lid and let the aroma of garlic and cumin and peppers waft across the steamy kitchen.

''Terrific,'' he muttered, then limped out of the room.

There was just time for her to shower and change into one of her newer pair of slacks and a matching honey-colored sweater before she heard his footsteps on the stairs.

''Those stairs are treacherous,'' he warned her.

Anny, ladling out two generous bowls of soup and topping them with a dollop of yogurt, nodded. ''The whole house is treacherous. Powder-post beetles have invaded it, the woodwork sprouts fungus whenever it rains, and the well water turns orange now and then with no warning.''

''I don't recall my lease mentioning orange water,'' Ty observed mildly, taking one of the trays and following her into the living room.

''There was no place on the form to work it in. Anyway, sometimes it doesn't happen for months in a row.'' Anny raked the coffee table clear and indicated Ty's space. ''About your shoes,'' she commenced.

''What about my shoes?''

"You need more support. I haven't suggested running because you need to work up to that sort of thing gradually, but you shouldn't even be walking in those things." She scooped the yogurt off her soup with a chunk of crusty brown bread, bit into it, and tucked her feet up onto the couch beside her.

"Look, Dr. Cousins, if it's all the same to you—"

"Of course, if you're determined to let yourself go to seed, there's nothing I can do about it. I'm no fitness fanatic, but I'm thirty-four, and common sense tells me that if I don't look after my basic equipment, in a few years I'm going to end up in the same shape as this house."

"Buggy, moldy, and falling apart." Ty grinned and extended his legs under the coffee table, displacing a pair and a half of shoes and a stack of books. There were always stacks of books and magazines beside the couch. If there was one thing he envied about his landlady, it was her library. He'd missed out on a lot of formal schooling as a boy, and he'd been making up for it ever since.

"At least you left off crooked and leaky," Anny observed dryly.

They scraped their soup bowls in companionable silence, and then, the informal meal finished, Anny held out her hands. "Let me see your foot. I just finished a great book on feet, and I think I can help you."

"A book on *feet*?" Amused, he complied, slipping the soft moccasin off and placing his sock-clad foot in her lap. "I'd like to look over this library of yours someday."

"Be my guest. Actually, it was something called foot reflexology." Removing the white wool sock with one hand, Anny gestured vaguely toward the adjoining room with the other. "Library's in there. There's no furniture except bookshelves, so you'll have to bring what you want in here or take them up to your room."

With strong, sure fingers, she began massaging his foot, exploring the calluses made by years of wearing fins. Thighs spread, Ty leaned back against the cushions at the other end of the couch and studied her under half-closed lids. After three weeks, she was more of an enigma than ever. Thirty-four, she'd said. A giggling girl one minute, a passionate woman the next; there was even something of the child about her—in her approach to life...as though life itself were the great adventure rather than any single aspect of it.

"How come you never married?" he asked pointblank.

Anny's fingers grew still for a moment, and then she went on working at the tender place on his heel. "I almost did...sort of. I guess I'm just not cut out to be a wife. How about you? Are you going to marry this Cass of yours?" She'd given him the message the same day she'd told him about her parents' impending visit. He'd agreed not to give away her status as landlady; he'd said nothing at all about Cass Valenti.

Nor did he now.

Ty was spending more and more time at the lab. The current project was a further study of high pressure nervous syndrome under varying compression rates and gas mixtures. Of the three participants, only Avery Fox was an experienced commercial diver. Lew Clifford was a biomedical specialist and George Jennings was a graduate student in the physics department. Ty eyed the golf ball, as the eight-foot spherical hyperbaric chamber in which the three men were enclosed was called, and wiped a film of perspiration from his forehead. He could actually feel the slight increase in his pulse rate as he recalled the last time he'd been closed up inside a similar space. It would be a hell of a thing if, after all his deep-sea experience, he finally succumbed to high pressure nervous syndrome at four hundred five feet *above* sea level.

The trouble was, he was literally a fish out of water. The lab, a three-floor complex that looked more like an elaborate boiler room than anything else, was the finest set-up of its kind anywhere in the world, but it just wasn't for him. He was more convinced of that with every day that passed.

Like all other oil rig divers, Ty had done his share of tending. For each diver below, there was always a tender on top to monitor every heartbeat and every breath, to regulate the flow and the mixture of gases, to sense potential problems before they became real ones. What he was doing here was not unlike what he'd done hundreds of times before, but there was one big difference: Out at sea, he could breathe. He could fill his lungs with good, fresh air, feel the wind and the sea spray on his body, the sun beating down on his head. Somewhere along the line that had become vitally important to him.

Ty turned his attention to the three men trapped inside the thick steel sphere. Jennings was going sour and they'd barely got underway. He was toughing it out, recording his own reactions, undergoing the physical and mental tests along with Fox and Clifford, but Ty had seen incipient panic enough times to recognize that glittery look in his eyes.

"Jennings reported mild visual and auditory hallucinations," Chuck Lyons, one of the navy physicians in attendance, observed. "Some nausea at oh-four-hundred, but that seems to have passed. Maybe he can shake it off."

"Maybe." Ty doubted it. So did Lyons, from his worried expression. No matter how carefully they screened the candidates for these simulated dives, there was always a chance of this happening. Currently under study was a better way of screening out potential victims of high pressure nervous syndrome as well as more effective ways of preventing it under actual extended dive conditions.

It was already dark by the time Ty left the campus. He drove more slowly than usual, his mind on automatic as he followed the twists and turns along the country roads. One thing had grown increasingly clear over the course of his stay at the environmental lab; the cloistered situation was not for him. Perhaps if he had the academic credentials to really be a part of what was going on, it would be different, but...

No, it wouldn't. It was a matter of temperament, and this didn't suit his. He found it suffocating. Ironically enough, each day he looked forward more and more to returning to Anny's place. The air there, while it wasn't exactly salty, was at least cool and clean and resinous. And it was there for the breathing.

Not like those poor devils trapped inside that overgrown Thermos bottle, living on a mixture of nitrogen, helium, and oxygen at about ten bucks a breath. They'd upped the nitrogen a few percent in an effort to counteract the hyperexcitability brought on by compression, but the increase might produce a narcotic effect in Fox and

Clifford. And it still might not be enough to help Jennings.

Ty remembered his first few experiences with deep, extended commercial dives. Back then, the mix had been straight helium and oxygen, a mix designed to keep a man sober. But at those depths, the gases inside the bell had to be kept so thick to keep the divers calm, that they had practically floated through the air. No matter what they ate, it was tasteless and chewy, and when they'd managed to sleep, the dreams...God, the dreams were incredible—and sometimes if you weren't even asleep, made you dreamed anyway. You sneezed, and the top of your head felt as if it was blowing off.

No, he was out of it now, and he wouldn't go back even if he could, not after backing off enough to get a little perspective. He'd been luckier than most, but luck could change. And he knew he couldn't go through what some of those poor devils went through—the muscle spasms, the cramps, the bloody hallucinations, the panic of knowing that there was no quick exit, the counting of every breath and wondering...wondering...

Anny was still in the studio when Ty came in. She'd forgotten to eat supper. Digging through copies of some of her early work, she'd come across a snow scene that, with minor modifications, could be turned into one bank of the Eno. She'd been working for six hours straight.

The door opened, and Ty stood there. He looked haggard.

"Hi, stranger," she greeted softly, arching her back against the stiffness. "Had anything to eat?"

"Yeah, I stopped off on the way home." It was a lie, but he couldn't face another cozy evening in her living room. He was tired as hell, and when he was tired, he couldn't always trust his judgment. Just lately, some of the ideas he'd been entertaining were a little too irrational for his peace of mind.

"Coffee?" She willed him to come closer, to approach the tall stool where she worked at her tilted drawing table.

"I'd better skip it, thanks. Your folks come tomorrow, right?"

Since he wasn't going to allow her to collapse into his arms, she slid off the stool and switched off her work light. "Right. Ty, I feel like an idiot about this, but you don't know my parents. If they had the slightest idea that their daughter was taking in roomers..."

"No problem. Am I a friendly roommate, or a live-in lover?" He slouched in the doorway, a twist of a smile carving deep lines in the sides of his face.

Anny held on to the edge of the table and fumbled her feet into her low suede boots. "Friend, I think, don't you? I'm no good at subterfuge." Her unruly mind came up with an attractive alternative, but reluctantly she dismissed it. If they became lovers, she wanted there to be no confusion as to the reason. "Look, it's crazy, I know, and I can't explain. Maybe you'll understand when you meet my parents. All I know is that it's important to me to keep peace with my family if I can do it without compromising my own standards."

Ty moved himself away from the doorframe. "Honey, don't sweat it. I've said I'll cooperate, and I will. What are friends for?"

His smile flicked over her eyes, her cheeks, and her lips, and then he was gone. Hearing the firm click of his door just down the hall, Anny capped her pen, sighed, and let herself out of the large, sparsely furnished studio.

She took time out from her work the next day to iron three dresses and attack her hair with a curling iron. She'd had to hunt through three rooms for the curler, finally locating it in a closet filled with bee gear and the dusty pint jars Hannibal had once used for his honey.

Ty took time out for a personal consultation with Chuck Lyons. The news was a mixture of good and bad, of hope and disappointment. His blood pressure, down from the last reading, hovered near normal. That was the good news. Spot readings throughout the working day, however, revealed a fluctuation that pegged him as a high risk personality.

"So I'm stuck with this thing," he'd concluded bitterly.

"Not necessarily," the wiry young officer replied. "I don't need to tell you what you're risking if you try any more dives. You're sweating it out with Jennings, aren't you? He goes into a spasm—your pressure shoots up. You're fighting for every breath as if you were inside that golf ball with him, aren't you?"

"And you're not?" Ty scoffed.

"I don't have your experiences behind me to trigger a physiological reaction. You guys put in a solid year of tending before you ever dive on a rig, don't you? I guess it's something you don't forget."

"There's a lot worth remembering, but a few things I'd just as soon forget." A wry smile lifted his grim expression for just a moment. "One thing I've learned—I'm not cut out for this dry-land diving. So what the hell am I going to do with the rest of my life? Weave baskets?"

"Wind up this session and get out of here. Learn to relax, learn to enjoy what you've got, instead of killing yourself for what you've lost."

It had been surprisingly easy after such an opening to get to the heart of what was really bothering him. Hesitantly at first, and then more confidently, Ty began to speak.

After a few minutes, the navy doctor leaned back and stroked his chin thoughtfully. "Why didn't you say so? These side reactions are pretty unpredictable. Some physicians don't mention the sexual side effects because apprehension can bring on the same results. You're afraid you can't; therefore you can't—if you know what I mean."

"Dammit, Chuck, I wasn't just running scared—I thought I could, but I couldn't."

"We'll switch you to another medication. Meanwhile, as soon as your time is up here, get yourself into a situation where you're comfortable and learn to relax. Stop pumping adrenaline and we'll see about cutting the dosage if you're still having problems with your sex life. You're the only one who can do it, man. All I can do is hand out pills and advice."

On his lunch hour, Ty got his new prescription filled. While he waited, he had himself fitted for a pair of shoes. Then, before he headed back to the lab, he stopped off for a sandwich: turkey on whole wheat, with a lot more greenery than he really cared for. Lifting his glass of skimmed milk in a silent toast, he smiled ruefully. Salud, *you witchy little baggage*.

Anny dried off hurriedly and slipped on one of Evan's older designs, a butterscotch cashmere. The steam from her stolen bath had relaxed her hair enough so it wasn't too bad. She'd lost what little knack she'd had with the curling iron, and besides that, there'd been traces of beeswax on the thing.

She heard Ty's car crunch on the gravel driveway and glanced hastily around his bathroom to make sure she'd left it in order. After a day like today, she simply hadn't been able to resist temptation. There was nothing like a hot soak to ease the tension brought about by working against a deadline, by her parents' arrival, and the injured redtail hawk that had been brought to her just before dark.

Ty came through the front door instead of using his own entrance. Anny was halfway down the stairs, shoes in her hands and a guilty look on her face. "I used your bathtub," she blurted out. "They're already here and they insisted on both of us for dinner, and then there was the redtail, and I truly didn't think you'd mind."

He stopped to stare at her, dropping the plastic carrier with his shoes onto the coffee table. "Out of that intriguing assortment, I think I'll go for the redtail first. Whose is it, yours? Would it be too indelicate to inquire as to how you came by it?"

Anny descended the remaining stairs, dropped her shoes on the floor, and walked on, not once taking her eyes from his face. Why was it that every time he came home, she found herself wanting to throw herself into his arms and pour out all her problems, her joys, and anything else pourable?

"It's a hawk," she explained. "A redtail hawk. I just got her a little while ago, and I'm not sure she's going to make it."

Hearing the note of real concern in her voice, Ty placed a hand on her shoulder. "Where is she? In the kitchen?"

"In a kennel carrier on the back porch. She was hit by a car."

"A *hawk*? I thought they were pretty high flyers."

"Yes, well, she'd just caught her supper, and she was flying along this narrow country road with thick, tall cedars on both sides—trying to get some altitude, I suppose. The rabbit she was carrying weighed almost as much as she did, and she couldn't turn loose in time to get away. Anyway, this pickup truck came barreling around a curve and hit her, and Ikey—that's the boy who was driving—brought her straight here. She was stunned, but I don't think anything's broken. My bird vet's gone for the weekend, so I put her in the carrier with a log to perch on. It'll keep her from thrashing around until I figure out what to do with her."

"Is there anything I can do?"

"I'm thawing half a dozen mice. I'll slip them into the carrier before we go," Anny murmured. "It's not a rabbit dinner, but it's the best I can come up with on short notice." Somehow, they'd come together in the middle of the room. Standing no more than a foot away, with that large, comforting hand on her shoulder, it was all she could do not to lean forward.

"Sort of potluck, you might say." Ty gazed down on top of her head. Funny, he'd never realized that leaf-brown hair could have such iridescent highlights. "I take it this is a coat-and-tie occasion?"

"The potluck, or my folks?" She was feeling better already. Funny how a person could draw strength from another person. It had never happened to her before, but then, she'd spent half her life learning to be her own source of strength.

Ty pressed his lips into her soft, wildflower-scented hair and then stood her away from him. "Give me ten minutes, will you? If you want to feed your new boarder while I shower, feel free. I'd just as soon pass on the first course."

Seven

Not since her engagement to Sidney Chambers had Anny subjected any man to her parents' tender mercies. Now, at the last moment, doubts began to creep in. "Look, it's not too late to make a run for it. They insisted you have dinner with us, but you can insist right back. I'll tell them you had a last-minute call from the lab."

Anny's anxious gaze took in the wine-colored silk tie and the superbly cut suit Ty wore so well. The strong desire she felt to show him off to her parents had nothing to do with the clothes he wore, but rather with the man he so obviously was. "They're really nice people, Ty, but you'd better brace yourself; either they'll dissect you, or they'll ignore you altogether, and let's face it, you're not an easy man to ignore. Honestly, they don't mean to be rude—it just comes out that way." Oh, this was going to be a terrific evening. Already she was feeling defensive on behalf of both parties.

"What did you tell them about us, anyway? Am I setting myself up as a target?" As they waited for the elevator to take them up to the suite Anny had booked for her parents, she plucked nervously at a loose button on the sleeve of her coat. It came off in her fingers, and she frowned at it absently until Ty took it from her and dropped it into his pocket.

"Are we supposed to be living together in the usual man-woman sense?" he persisted.

Her reply came just a shade too quickly. "Lord, no! I told them—well, nothing, really. Just that you were staying with me for a while. I wouldn't have mentioned you at all, but Claire thought you were an owl, and one thing led to another." She gave him an apologetic look. "You're safe enough from bodily harm. I assured Claire you were just a friend. We agreed, didn't we? And anyway, Evan's not the shotgun type."

"You always call them by their given names?"

Anny shrugged and stepped into the elevator. "Their choice. You'll understand better when you meet them." She was acutely conscious of Ty's eyes on her averted face as the doors swished shut. What was he thinking? That her hair was too curly? That the evening promised to be an enormous bore? That in a few short days he'd be entering another hotel with another woman?

And with another purpose in mind, she reminded herself with brutal diligence.

Three hours later, as the four of them sat over the ruins of a superb dinner, Anny wondered why she'd expected things to be any different just because Ty was with her.

They still treated her as if she were fifteen and none too bright.

"Annabelle, you look so...sweet," Claire had greeted, brushing her flawless, perennially tanned cheek a fraction of an inch away from Anny's. "I had no *idea* you still had that old dress. Still, it holds its style remarkably well, I must say. Evan, what do you think? Is that the same line Corrinne used for her Saint Tropez collection? I told you she didn't have an original idea in her head."

Evan Cousins, dressed as always to complement his deep tan and his carefully casual pewter-colored hair, examined the dress with cool, critical eyes. He reached out and yanked off the belt, then nodded approvingly. "Lose ten pounds. It should flow from the shoulders, break just here"—he slashed at her hipbone with a manicured karate chop—"and sweep to the lower calf. The shoes are hideous. Get rid of the breasts and get yourself some—"

"Daddy!"

"Oh. Sorry, love, force of habit. How are you, and how's this young man of yours?" Evan's polished smile of apology wavered ever so slightly as he looked up—and up and up—to meet Tyrus's flinty eyes. "Evan Cousins here. Delighted to meet you."

With reservations at eight-thirty, they'd allowed time for drinks in the suite first. Time for Claire, lovely as always in winter white, to launch a barrage of outrageous questions. She'd gone the oblique route at first, but Ty was more than a match for her. A mention of the United Daughters of the Confederacy brought forth a tale about a Confederate gunboat he'd dived on, and the Daughters of the American Revolution elicited a similar response.

Evan was drinking too much, Anny noted. Now on his third whiskey-and-soda, he stared first at Anny and then at Ty. An errant thought drifted through Anny's mind, and her lips trembled on a smile. Maybe she'd spoken too quickly about the shotgun. And then the urge to smile fled as once again she felt herself awash in a familiar, frustrating sea of helplessness, resentment, and love.

Why am I sitting here listening to a recital of Mom's illustrious ancestors and Daddy's gold-plated clients when I should be home with my hawk?

"...picked up this *marvelous* cutwork in this *marvelous* little out-of-the-way place. Holmes's yacht was almost as large as the whole island. The poor woman simply didn't know what she had! Nikki bought her out for practically nothing, and we found hordes more on the other islands, all with this same funny little motif. Evan's doing a whole line around it."

We should be seated around my kitchen table now, with Daddy carving and Mama fussing about my table setting, and Ty getting up to put another log in the fireplace.

Claire, her cobalt eyes guileless, launched a direct surprise attack. "I believe Annabelle mentioned that you're on the faculty at Duke? Which department is that?"

"I'm not on the faculty, Mrs. Cousins. I'm there for a one-shot project."

"Call me Claire, please. And what is it exactly that you do for a living?" The eyes remained wide in their bed of dense, navy blue lashes.

"I recently retired."

"How...fascinating," Claire murmured. "From what?"

"From salvage diving."

Anny thought she detected a thread of amusement in Ty's tone, as though he were playing a game of his own invention. She only hoped his sense of humor held out. Any minute now the conversation would move on from his prospects to his intentions toward their daughter.

"*Salvage* diving? What an *odd* occupation. Your family is in...uh...salvage?" The word, on Claire's lips, sounded more like garbage.

Anny stared at the delicate design in the damask tablecloth and vowed never to subject another man to this genteel inquisition. A pleasant evening with her parents—was that too much to expect? She was thirty-four years old, not a teen-ager off on her first date. Besides which, she'd introduced Ty as a friend, not a contender for her hand in marriage.

"My father was in shipping," Ty replied smoothly. "Unfortunately, my family broke up while I was still a boy, and I don't really remember him very well."

To his credit, he never revealed the slightest hint of impatience. Anny gave him high marks for that. He carried his end of the conversation, and hers as well, for the most part. Several times, as if guessing that her thoughts were back at home with the injured hawk, he reached for her hand under the table. Even that small gesture, Anny suspected, did not go unnoticed by Claire.

Allowing the balm of his deep, resonant voice to flow over her, Anny toyed with her heavy silver dessert spoon. She'd owe him for this. Foot massages, the freedom of her library, breakfast for the rest of his stay. Whatever she could do to make the remainder of his time with her more pleasant, she promised herself to do it cheerfully. Not that it would entail any big sacrifice on her part, she admitted, her face softening in a tiny private smile.

"Anny? Come back to earth, darling."

Claire's penetrating voice scattered a flurry of warm pink thoughts, and Anny felt Ty's hand close over her thigh under the table, his touch silently supportive. She beamed at him and then turned a questioning look on her mother.

"I said, why don't you run up to New York with us? While Evan's seeing all the people he has to see, you and I can get started on some serious shopping. It's time you turned your closets out and started fresh, from the skin out. That coat of yours is a disgrace, for one thing, and your father's right about those shoes. That heel just isn't worn this season."

Anny felt under the table for her maligned shoes, herding them protectively between her stockinged feet. "They're good shoes," she defended.

"I'm not going to take no for an answer. If money's the problem, then say no more; you won't have to spend a penny. Remember, darling, you'll never get anywhere in this world unless you dress the part. It's been proven scientifically over and over again," Claire announced with the conviction of one who never adulterated her opinions with mere fact.

One, two, three, four, five, six... "Claire, I couldn't possibly get away now."

Claire's speculative gaze went from Ty to Anny, then back again. "Of course, I understand, dear. Tyrus can come, too. Surely this little project of his can be postponed for a few days? We'll shop all of one day and then take in a few shows and a few parties. All the fun people will be there."

The party broke up soon after that, with the New York trip still hanging. Somehow, Anny's repeated negative answers got swallowed up in Claire's enthusiasm until she could barely speak past the constriction in her throat. *They're your parents,* she reminded herself over and over. *In spite of everything, they* do *love you, and you love them!*

She made arrangements to meet them in Durham the following afternoon. Ty begged off, claiming pressure of work. After a round of delicate embraces and a few embarrassingly pointed remarks about Anny's improved taste in *some* areas, Anny and Ty hurried outside. Once safely on the road home, she made a deliberate effort to calm herself.

"I'm sorry, Ty, sorry I put you through all that business. Why I thought it would make a difference, I'll never know—your being along, I mean." She uttered a short laugh. "Hoping for a miracle, I suppose. Hoping that for once, they'd see me as an adult. Your little project, indeed! As if you could hang out a 'gone fishing' sign and take off, just like that! And did it ever occur to them that I work for a living, too? That I can't just pick up and dash out of town when the whim strikes? Did either of them even ask what I was working on now?"

It had been a foolish dream, and she'd thought she'd outgrown dreams. She'd been so proud when she'd landed the job with Persimmon Press, and soon afterward, when she'd taken Sid to meet her parents. He was attractive, intelligent, and he'd recently been made a full professor at the university. It hadn't made a speck of difference; they'd simply ignored him.

"Well, no one could ever ignore *you,*" she muttered belligerently. "But, dammit, I hate feeling guilty!"

Ty ignored the nonsequitur. He was learning that to understand Anny, one listened to what she meant, not to what she said. "What do you have to feel guilty about? Incidentally, they didn't buy it—the platonic business."

"I know. I'm sorry about that, too. I'm sorry about everything." She threw up her hands. "Don't ask me why I always feel so guilty after one of their visits; I just do." Reclining against the deep comfort of the leather seat, she slipped off her shoes and stroked the soft carpet with the soles of her feet. "They didn't want a child, they wanted a doll, a pretty toy they could take out of the box and show off and then put away again. Instead, they got a colicky baby who threw up on Daddy's twelve-hundred-dollar suit and cried all through her own christening. I didn't improve with age, either," she added almost defiantly. "I ate my way through a perfectly miserable adolescence and wore a size fourteen when I was thirteen. Even after I shot up and trimmed down, I was a mess."

Ty's comfortable silence drew forth feelings she'd never put into words before, and Anny rambled on. "There are five of them now, you know—Evan's boutiques, that is, and they're all at the very best addresses. Evan never has any trouble finding backers, no matter what the rest of the economy is like. I used to wish they'd all fail except one, and we could stay in one place for a whole year. How's that for an excuse to feel guilty?"

"If you're going to crucify yourself for past wishes, wait until you've lined up enough to make it worthwhile."

Toes curling into the plush carpeting, Anny continued to stare unseeingly at the tall pines that flickered hypnotically alongside the dark highway. "We had two condos and a house, and we migrated like geese. In between, there were trips to Europe, cruises with Evan's business friends—Evan doesn't have any other kind of friends—

and sometimes they took me along if there was someone to look after me."

"Poor little rich kid," Ty taunted, but it was a gentle taunt, and Anny couldn't take offense.

"Actually, I don't think we were all that rich. We just managed to live that way. Evan's talent and Claire's connections. The trouble was, we never slowed down long enough for me to discover who I was and where I belonged. I kept looking for something real, but it was all so perfect. The greens and pools and courts, the gardens, and even the riding trails. Did you know that the bridle trails are swept every morning and evening in some places so that the riders won't be offended by the sight of manure?"

Examining his strong, irregular profile, she waited for a comment. Was he even listening? Probably not. *Hopefully* not, she amended. "I used to imagine that it was all a stage set. Leaves never withered and died, flowers never faded. They were all clipped off in the dead of night and whisked away, and in the morning, when the pedigreed dogs were walked by pedigreed owners wearing pedigreed resort wear, a stagehand hurried after them with a tiny scoop. But, of course, the pups were all *much* too well bred to commit an indiscretion. And certainly no mongrels were permitted onstage."

She huddled into her coat, gazing into the past and marveling at the imagination of an unhappy child. "I used to want to run away and find out where the stage ended and the real world began."

"And did you ever find it?"

"I think so," she replied quietly. The steady hum of the engine created a sense of isolation, of security, and Anny eased her seatbelt and twisted to tuck her knees on the seat beside her. "Of course I did. It's really ironic, you know. I did exactly what Evan had done when he was my age. I took my life into my own hands and shaped it into what I wanted it to be, which is probably why I feel so guilty. I'm happy doing what I do, Ty. I like my life, but it doesn't include any of the things Claire and Evan consider important. And I *hate* knowing that they look on me as deprived."

"Deprived." Ty tasted the word experimentally. "Somehow, that's not a word I'd ever associate with you, Anny."

"You might if you spent too much time with Claire. I always come away with my thinking all screwed up, and it takes forever to get myself sorted out again. Once when I was about twelve, I heard one of the maids telling another one about her new carpet. She said it was brown tweed, because she had four kids. Ty, we always had white carpets. No matter where we were, Palm Springs or Palm Beach or wherever, we had white carpets. That's not reality—reality is brown tweed."

The tenor of the tires changed as they left the highway for the rougher country road. Anny allowed her eyes to close for a moment, and then forgot to open them. Ty, glancing across to where she sat curled up like a wilting flower, smiled in the darkness. Let her sleep. He was beginning to understand a lot of what made Anny who she was. Odd that they should have come from such different beginnings and ended up living together in the backwoods of North Carolina in perfect harmony.

At least there was no guilt involved in his own case. He'd done his best for the one parent he'd known, and when she was beyond his help, he'd helped himself. He owed nothing to any man. As far as he knew, he'd hurt no one along the way. Whatever he decided to do in the future, with Cass or without her, he had enough in the way of investments to keep them off the streets. The sort of diving he'd done for so long paid extremely well, and he'd had no one to spend money on. A man could only throw away so much in pursuit of happiness and still stay fit enough to go on working.

"Wake up, honey," he whispered, switching off the engine. The tick of cooling metal broke the stillness of the night, and Anny stirred.

"I talk too much, don't I?" she murmured, fumbling for the buckle of her seatbelt. Reaching across her, he unsnapped it and eased it from her shoulders, his hands gentle, if impersonal, as they brushed across her breasts. "You've really served above and beyond the call of duty tonight, Ty. I appreciate it."

"My pleasure. What about your shoes?"

She slipped them on, her thoughts turning to the injured hawk. "It's getting colder. Maybe I'd better throw a rug over the carrier just for tonight. I don't want to startle her so that she thrashes around, but if she were covered, perhaps she'd feel less threatened tomorrow."

Ty followed her inside and locked up behind them, a small homey gesture that made her feel somehow weepy. *Not now, you idiot! You've embarrassed the man enough for one night.*

Besides, she needed an early night to clear her head. The mews hadn't been used in some time; first thing tomorrow, she'd need to get it ready for its new occupant. "Ty, thanks for going along with the command performance. You didn't have to, but I'm glad you did. Otherwise, I'd have had to invent a biography and answer all sorts of personal questions about you."

"I did a bit of inventing, myself. Sorry about that; it just seemed to be called for at the time."

"What part was invention? The places you've visited?"

"Worked, not visited. There's a big difference, and no, it was that business about my father."

"You mean he's not in shipping?" She hadn't questioned it at the time. The car he drove, the clothes he wore, the subtle air of command that was so much a part of his very nature, even when he was reclining on her sofa having his foot massaged, all indicated a cosmopolitan background.

"He probably was, in a manner of speaking. I never knew which one of the merchant seamen who stopped off at the boardinghouse where my mother worked fathered me. I narrowed it down to two candidates, but since my mother named me for both of them, I'm not sure she knew, either." For the first time all night, he was aware of the old tension, and it irritated him. So he was the bastard son of a hard-working woman who hadn't laughed a lot, and who'd been described by one of his grade-school teachers as being "no better than she should be." As a boy, he'd puzzled long hours over the phrase. And Anny's was a background of posh resorts and exclusive schools, with a family on her mother's side that predated the Constitution.

Anny was no snob. And even if she were, what the hell did he care?

But he did. He cared very much what she thought of him, and that knowledge only increased his irrational anger.

"Tyrus." Her soft voice broke through the surface tension of his thoughts. "I wondered about that. Isn't

there a river named the Tyrus, too? No, that's the Ti-
gris. So what were your fathers' names?''

Ty's ragged sigh of resignation drained the anger from
him as swiftly as it had arisen, and he slipped his arms
around her, brushing his chin across her hair. ''You're a
nice woman, Anny Lee Cousins. One of my fathers was
named Tyler and the other one was Russell.''

''Tyrus. It describes you. Mine's actually Annabelle
LeMontrose Cousins, only Cousins is really Koscienski,
but Evan had it legally changed. Nothing is ever what it
seems, is it?'' Sighing, she buried her face in the warmth
of his shirtfront and inhaled the scent of good woolens,
subtle cologne, and healthy male flesh. ''Maybe that's
why it took me so long to find what was real for me.''

''And you found it here with all your owls and mice
and bees and hawks,'' Ty said softly, his breath setting
flyaway strands dancing about her cheekbones.

''Speaking of which, I'd better go drape something
over the carrier. I hope she's eaten at least a little bit.
Normally, a redtail will eat her weight in food every day,
but under the circumstances, she might not have touched
a bite.'' The hawk's need for additional protection was
probably not as great as Anny's need to protect and nur-
ture, to be needed. All the same, it wouldn't hurt to check
on her once before morning.

''Need any help?''

Reluctantly, Anny disengaged herself. ''Thanks, but
any human contact is bad enough. I try to keep it to a
minimum. I'll put the carrier in the mews tomorrow if
she's better, and take her to the vet as soon as he gets
back to town. Meanwhile, I'd probably better see if I can
get a few pigeons.''

"I notice you didn't order the squab tonight," Ty teased.

"And I notice you ate all your salad and ignored the salt shaker," she countered, on her way to the back door.

"Maybe I decided to follow your advice and get myself back in shape."

"This sudden spurt of good behavior wouldn't have anything to do with your friend Cass, I suppose."

Ty's eyes grew wary. "In what way?"

Confused, Anny shook her head. "I only thought— well, you certainly look a lot more relaxed these past few weeks. At least you don't bite first and bark afterward. Or does Cass like the tough-guy approach?"

He turned toward the stairs. Glancing over his shoulder, he dismissed his suspicions. "Yeah, well..." Shrugging, he allowed a grudging grin to break through. "I guess I was in a pretty foul mood when I first got here. Cass and I had...uh...had a few words. This hypertension thing had me worried, coming along with everything else. Think she'll see an improvement?"

"In your disposition? Definitely." Anny turned away, anger churning inside her for no good reason at all. She'd never hated anyone in her life, but if that woman hurt this man...!

Marching across the kitchen, Anny decided that she disliked Cass Valenti on general principle.

Ty continued up the stairs, his mind already focused on the coming meeting. He'd been rehearsing it in his mind ever since Cass had mentioned the possibility of a trip to Raleigh. Each night he'd gone to bed with her image before him. But the image of black glossy hair, of impudent eyes and taunting red lips, he admitted reluctantly, kept getting tangled up with another image.

Anny. She was as different from Cass as day from night, and yet in her own unique way, she was attractive. Damnably attractive. He'd noticed that right away, even when he'd been scared, mad as hell, and still sore at women in general.

At the door to his bedroom, he paused. It wasn't his disposition that worried him. Where Cass was concerned, there was only one area of importance between them. If he let her down again, there wouldn't be another chance.

He heard the sound of a door opening and closing downstairs as he took off his jacket and hung it over the back of a chair. The tie followed, and he began on the buttons of his shirt, his mind suspended somewhere between the evening behind him and the exciting nights in store. He'd just unfastened his belt when he heard the kitchen door open again. It closed quickly, and then there was silence. Eyes narrowed, he tilted his head in a listening stance as some instinct born of years of experience both as a diver and a tender, of being totally aware of every nuance of atmospheric change, alerted him. Quietly he rebuckled his belt, leaving his shirt hanging open.

She was standing in the middle of the room when he reached her, her arms hanging limply at her sides as she stared out the dark window. One look at her face was all it took. Moving swiftly, Ty gathered her unresisting form into his arms. "Ah, honey, I'm sorry, I'm sorry," he murmured.

Ty tried to feel what she was feeling, to take her pain onto his own shoulders, but he'd never known what it was like to have a pet. And this wasn't even a pet, but a wild bird someone had dumped on her back porch a few hours ago. "Anny, Anny, there's nothing you could have done."

Anny accepted the gesture for what it was meant to be. How could he understand her grief when she herself couldn't understand? So beautiful, so wild, so frightened, her lady hawk...she'd lived by the laws of nature, harming no man.

Anny felt cold all over. She shivered in Ty's arms, and his hands came up to hold her face away, his gaze, dark with concern, taking in her dry eyes and the droop of her mouth.

"Cry, then, little love, cry if it'll help," he whispered, never even wondering at the source of such tenderness.

"It'll only hurt for tonight. I'll be all right by tomorrow." The sound of distance was in her voice, as though already she were seeing past the pain, accepting the patterns of endings and beginnings. She could have as easily mourned for the rabbit, for the pigeons, or the mice. Life was more than white carpets, and for every bit of grief, Hannibal had taught her, there was a corresponding joy.

Ty brushed a calloused fingertip across her cheek, as if the tears had been visible. In silence, they held on to one another, and gradually he became aware of a resonance deep inside him, a sense of rightness that he didn't even try to understand.

Her voice muffled against his shoulder, Anny spoke. "Could I ask one more favor of you, Ty? Would you sleep with me tonight?"

Eight

I can't believe I said that," Anny whispered in hushed agony. She waited for Tyrus to laugh. Or to push her away. "Ty, I didn't mean that the way it sounded," she rushed in earnestly, "or rather, I *did*—but I didn't. I mean about sleeping."

Tearing herself from his arms, she plopped down into a kitchen chair and buried her face in her hands. "Oh, you know what I mean," she finished with a despairing groan.

Ty, his feet braced apart, stared down at her helplessly. What the hell was going on? A bird died, a woman cried—or didn't cry, which was somehow worse—and his gut got all twisted up in knots. What the devil was there about this crazy female that affected him this way? This was no time to get mixed up with her emotional hang-ups, not with Cass arriving in a couple of days. It was bad enough that her visit was coming at a time when things were coming to a head at the lab. With one last chance to redeem himself in Cass's eyes, he couldn't afford any additional distractions.

"Anny..." He stared down at the top of her head and allowed himself a single small distraction. Those iridescent highlights that danced on the surface of her light brown hair, that wild tangle of curls that sailed off at an angle... Bless her, she'd done something to it, but somehow he didn't think it had come out quite the way it was supposed to.

Taking the soft, disobedient tendril in his hand, he tugged gently. "Anny, go put on your pajamas and bathrobe and I'll make us some hot tea with milk, all right?"

Too emotionally drained to argue, Anny obeyed, her footsteps dragging as she opened the door to her icy bedroom. The knob on the heat register had broken off in the shut position years ago, and she'd never bothered to have it repaired. She slept better in a cold room anyway.

The tea was lukewarm, and Ty apologized. He led her into the living room, where he'd put a split log on the coals in the fireplace, seated her on the couch with an afghan over her lap, and handed her the brimming mug. Then he sat down across from her and watched, his gaze anxious under heavy, dark brows. "Is it okay? Is it too weak? The honey wouldn't come out of that squeeze thing, so I didn't sweeten it much."

"It's fine, just lovely. It's the cold weather." Anny swallowed the tepid, tasteless beverage and managed to smile. Tomorrow she'd show him the pan for heating the milk.

"The cold weather," Ty repeated, nodding as though he knew exactly what she was talking about.

"I usually keep in on the hearth, but I forgot. It's wonderful the way things just mesh together, isn't it?" she added with brittle vivacity. "Nature's plan. In the summer there are ants and you can't, but you don't need to, and in the winter when you do, the ants are gone, so you can."

Ty nodded again. There was a thread of logic in there somewhere, but for the moment it escaped him. "Anny, do you have any tranquilizers?"

"For what?" She stared at him blankly.

"For...well, to help you get to sleep."

Anny clanked her mug down on the coffee table. "Ty, I don't need any pills. There's nothing in the world wrong with me, except that I'm tired and a little sad, and I just thought it might be nice to fall asleep in the arms of—of a friend." *A friend!* Her emotions flayed raw by the events of the past few hours, Anny no longer had the strength to avoid facing facts. Perhaps her innocent request had not been so innocent, after all. What she wanted from Tyrus Clay was far more than friendship, but if friendship was all he could offer, she'd have to settle for that. Wouldn't she? Hadn't she always?

"Anny, do you have any brandy in the house?"

"No, but I think there's some moonshine around here somewhere. I have a friend who supplements his Social Security by curing hams and making whiskey. Did you know that touching is good for what ails you?" She hurried on in an attempt to explain away her inept proposition. "According to an article I read recently, touching actually stimulates the body's own restorative processes." Leveling a direct challenge, she added, "You didn't seriously think I had anything else in mind, did you?"

He had, as a matter of fact, and it had scared the hell out of him. From the signals his body had been sending out lately, his troubles on that score were largely a thing of the past, but when a man had failed repeatedly, and then been ridiculed for his efforts, it left him gun shy. Besides, there was Cass. "Of course I didn't, honey, I know you better than that. Still feeling rocky? A drink might not be a bad idea."

"The radiator they used to make the whiskey was probably soldered with lead." Even without the risk of lead poisoning from an improperly made still, Anny had no intention of muddling her thought processes still further with alcohol. With the help of the wine they'd consumed with dinner, she'd been maudlin enough for one night. The lack of any real closeness with her parents always depressed her, but it was certainly nothing new. As for the hawk, she'd known losses before; she would again. Working with wild birds, she'd had to learn to accept her losses along with her triumphs. It didn't make the losses any less painful, but Anny prided herself on being a realist.

If she was falling apart—and she was—it was all Ty's fault. She'd been happy enough in her comfortable rut until he'd come along and plowed it all up. Unfortunately, she'd made the mistake of thinking herself invulnerable, hardly a proper attitude for an avowed pragmatist.

When had it started? When had she fallen in love with him? That first day, when he'd presented her with such an irresistible challenge? Physically, the man was pure dynamite. When he'd announced the fact that he was *not* a happy man, nor a genial one, and warned her to keep her distance...

Well, what could she do? It had been an open invitation to someone long accustomed to rehabilitating the wildest of wild creatures. Only she hadn't meant to involve her heart. Somewhere along the line, she'd dropped her guard for just an instant, and that was all it had taken. The funny part was, she hadn't even realized that she'd *had* a guard.

Deliberately lifting her gaze to meet those hooded, flint-gray eyes, Anny felt the hard edge of sadness begin to crumble away as a tide of warmth swept through her. "Ty, go to bed," she urged gently. "Stop fussing around like a broody hen with one chick. It was that last glass of wine, that's all. Sometimes it affects me this way. I'll snap back as good as new after a night's sleep."

His sharp eyes took in everything about her in a single practiced sweep. First off, she was too pale. Her skin was the sort that probably never tanned, but she was paler than usual tonight, her few freckles standing out in bold relief. Add to that the shadows around her eyes, the stubborn set of her jaw, and it told a story. The woman was physically exhausted, emotionally wiped out, but for some reason she felt compelled to pretend she was all right.

If he knew Anny, she was already regretting her lapse in asking him to sleep with her. She wouldn't take pills, she refused to drink to help her relax, and she couldn't even let herself cry.

He shook his head in frustrated admiration. What do you do with a woman who's too proud to ask for help, and too innately honest to deny that she needs it? Reluctantly, he left her there, after making her promise to go to bed as soon as she'd finished her tea.

An hour later, no nearer to sleep than before, he swore softly into the darkness. "Dammit to hell, why won't she *cry*? If she'd just bawl her head off for a few minutes, she'd feel better." God knows there'd been plenty of times when he'd wished he could cry. A man got as clogged up emotionally as a woman, only as a rule, the pain was buried under too many layers of machismo ever to see the light of day.

He rolled over, pulling the covers with him and swore again when the cold air struck his naked backside. He'd bet his last dollar that there wasn't a scrap of insulation in those walls. The first floor was little better. Every time the wind blew, it rearranged all the seed heads and dried weeds she had jammed into jars all over the house.

Crazy woman! He'd met a few eccentrics in his time, but Anny Cousins could hold her own with the best of them. Yet, with it all—the zany ideas, the way she had of talking in riddles, those peculiar clothes she wore—he couldn't deny that she was both capable and caring, and both stimulating and relaxing. And he had to admit that she was one of the most beautiful women he'd ever seen. Beautiful on her own terms. Beautiful enough, he added, moving restlessly on the rumpled sheets, to get him steamed up without even trying. He had a feeling Anny wasn't going to be easy to forget.

Downstairs, the wheezing old mantel clock struck six, which meant it was four o'clock. When he'd tackled her on that one, she'd come back with her own brand of irrefutable logic.

"But I know what it means, so what difference does it make what it says?"

Sitting up, Ty stroked his jaw thoughtfully. He knew what *she* meant, so what difference did it make what she'd said?

Stepping into a pair of jeans, he tiptoed to the head of the stairs, oblivious to the icy floor and the freezing gusts that rattled the windowpanes at either end of the hall. The light was still on in the living room. He'd been right, then; she was still there. She'd needed a friend, and he'd deliberately ignored her signals because he'd been afraid to tempt fate.

She was asleep on the couch, her neck bent at an awkward angle, both bare feet protruding from the skimpy afghan. The fire had long since gone out.

"Oh, hell," he growled, bending to scoop her up into his arms. Trailing bathrobe, afghan, and a corner of the morning paper, he shouldered his way into her bedroom, flinching at the rush of frigid air. No wonder she hadn't wanted to come in here; he'd seen warmer refrigerators!

Thinking longingly of the electric blanket on his bed upstairs, Ty settled her onto one side of the double bed, easing the bathrobe off and spreading it on top of the layered quilts. He stared down at her for a long moment, seeing the fine silken tangle of her hair across the pillow, the blue shadows around her eyes.

She looked so incredibly vulnerable...so alone. A woman shouldn't be alone. Hell, a man shouldn't be alone, either, for that matter. Thinking of what she'd said about touching, he sighed. In a few days, he'd no longer be alone. He'd have Cass again.

But what about Anny? Long after he'd finished up here and gone back to the coast, Anny would be here alone, working too late into the night, not bothering to stop and eat, walking too far into the woods with no one to know or care if she got home safely. Even the wild, injured birds she filled her life with didn't bear touching. Except for the hatchlings, human contact, especially at feeding time, was avoided. She didn't even have the comfort of a pet.

Leaning over, he tucked the quilts around her neck. If she had only one electric blanket, why didn't she use it herself instead of giving it to him?

Anny stirred restlessly and slipped one bare foot outside the covers. She muttered something under her breath, and a soft frown gathered like crumpled velvet on her brow.

Ty shushed her. Then, swearing silently, he crawled in with her, gasping as the cold sheets touched his bare back. He'd stay only until she was sleeping soundly, he told himself. All she'd asked of him was a pair of comforting arms; he could certainly offer her that much, after all the interest she'd taken in his welfare.

Besides, his conscience wouldn't allow him to go back upstairs to his electric blanket knowing she was shivering down here under half a ton of quilts. Quilts didn't generate any heat. Ty knew enough about the human heating system to know that there were times when it needed a boost.

Anny snuggled her back into his front as confidently as if she'd slept with a "friend" every night of her life, and Ty, feeling the immediate physiological reaction he was coming to associate with her nearness, braced himself for a long night. Resigned to his fate, he wrapped an arm around her waist and drew her closer. If a little holding was good for the human condition, maybe they'd both benefit from a spot of closeness.

Her hair tickled his lips and her perfume assaulted his nostrils. One of her ice-cold feet wedged its way between his, seeking warmth. As he settled himself more comfortably, it occurred to Ty that this was probably the first time in his life he'd deliberately gone to bed with a woman in his arms with no thought of making love to her before the night was over.

Sometime before dawn, Ty finally slept. His dreams were wildly erotic, and when someone attempted to drag him up from the womb of sleep, he resisted as long as he could.

"Ty, wake up!"

It was Anny. Somehow, she'd managed to escape from the tantalizing landscape of his dream and now she was trying to pull him away, too. "Come back where you belong," he muttered, drawing her back against his hungry flesh without ever opening his eyes.

"Ty, you don't—"

"Yes, I do," he purred against her ear, and then he caught the lobe between his teeth and nipped. Somehow, her pajama top had come unfastened, and his finger trailed circles around her breast, circles that mounted higher and higher as they neared their goal.

Anny struggled to get away, but her struggles were curiously weak as she attempted to sort out dream from reality. She'd awakened to find herself in bed with a fully aroused man, one of his hands stroking her bare breast and the other one fumbling at the waistband of her flannel pajamas. Every nerve ending in her body was on fire, inflamed by the most vivid dreams she'd ever experienced in her life.

Oh, Lord, no wonder he was aroused! What had she been *doing* to him in her sleep? What was *he* doing to *her*? "Ty, what are you doing in my bed?"

"I should think that's pretty obvious." His hand slid under the elastic waistband to stroke the soft plane below her waist. He pushed the barrier of cotton down over her hips, and Anny snatched it back up again, her defense curiously inept. A few moments later, the flannel was a warm, rumpled knot at the foot of the bed.

Ty's fingertips began a thorough exploration of the terrain, from the delicate ridges of her hipbones, down the hammock of her belly, lingering at the tiny crater of her navel, and dipping dangerously near the soft tangle of silk Anny guarded with updrawn knees.

A shuddering breath caught in her throat as she felt her resistance seeping away. Of course she was still dreaming. She had to be. In a little while she'd wake up alone, as always.

No, dammit, she *wasn't* asleep! And this had gone far enough. "Ty, listen to me, this is all wrong," she whispered desperately, plucking his fingers from her thigh only to have them steal around to her breast.

She flounced over onto her back and twisted her head around to glare at him. His hair, that soft, crisp pelt of ebony, glinted with random threads of silver, looking more windblown than slept-in. His eyes were closed. The sunburned tips of his dark lashes feathered across his cheeks, inviting her touch. And he was *smiling*!

"Nothing that feels so right can be too wrong," he murmured. "Now, let's go back to the beach and pick up where we left off. The sun's shining, the water's as clear as pale green air, and I'm waiting in the shallows. You've just dived over the side of the launch, and I'm watching you swim ashore. Did you know your breasts float up when you tread water?''

"Tyrus!" Had he been dreaming the same sort of dream she had? The scoundrel was playing with her, trying to make her think he didn't know what he was doing. She was tempted to go along with him, just to see how far he'd go.

"Ah, you're wading ashore now, right into my arms...so lovely, with the salt water beading up like diamonds all over your body and your hair streaming down your back.''

Was that really reverence she heard in his voice—or was it laughter? "My hair's too short to stream anywhere," she pointed out, trying to ignore the return of his hand to her breast.

"We'll let it grow, love. I'm going to kiss every salt diamond from your body, starting with your lips, hmm?''

"Ty, you're being absurd!" Her breathless protest duly registered, Anny gave herself up to his kiss. One kiss couldn't cause much damage, could it? After all, they were both still dreaming, both half asleep.

But it was no dream kiss that laid bare her very soul, that kindled fires that had been waiting forever for the spark of life. He pulled her tightly against him, stroking her back, shaping her hips in his palm and pressing her achingly close to his throbbing body.

"Oh, Anny, I need you," he groaned, lifting his mouth from hers to kiss her eyes, her cheeks, her chin. "You don't know how much I—''

Oh, yes, oh, yes, please, darling.

Had she actually said it? Had she spoken the words, or was she still in a dream, still lying in the crystal shallows, her naked body burning from the kiss of the sun, from the fevered kisses of a dream lover?

Her head was cradled on one of his arms, and reluctantly Ty dragged the other one slowly up her body to stroke her hair away from her face. His eyes were open now. Hers were closed, and he gave in to one last temptation and kissed the softly shadowed lids.

God, he ought to be shot! This was Anny, not some bimbo he'd picked up for the price of a few drinks. Just because he'd gotten himself straightened out again and the old appetites were ravening, that was no excuse to take advantage of someone like Anny. She'd needed a friend, not a quick tumble. In a moment of stress, she'd turned to him for comfort, and he'd been about to betray that trust, that friendship.

"Honey, I'd better get out of here before we both get in over our heads." He eased himself away, fighting a guilty conscience and frustrated desire.

As he watched, her lashes fluttered, but her eyes stayed shut. She was hiding. It was all he could do not to gather her in his arms again and let nature take its course. He'd never felt so confused in his life. The trouble was, she did such crazy things to him! He'd never felt this way about any woman before, and it just didn't add up. Not when there was Cass, the woman he'd hungered for so insatiably ever since she'd kicked him out of her life.

He was halfway out of bed when the phone rang. Never had the shrill summons come at a more welcome time. Snapping his jeans, Ty hit the deck running, slamming the door behind him.

Anny huddled in a fetal coil, eyes open to the pale light filtering into the room. From just outside her bedroom, she could hear the rumble of Ty's voice, and she waited for him to call her. It would be Claire, wanting to know about the New York trip.

Damn New York, damn Ty, and damn her for setting herself up! Had he ever so much as hinted that he might be falling in love with her? Of course not. Whatever he had going with Cass obviously took precedence over any nebulous relationship that might have been growing between them. Oh, he'd wanted her, all right. Whatever had prompted him to climb into bed with her in the first place—lust, misguided sympathy—that much had been unmistakable.

But had he even given her a chance to decide whether she wanted him or not? He had not! He'd knocked down every shred of resistance she'd managed to muster, and then, when she was a throbbing, quivering mass of need, he'd backed down.

Had she done something to turn him off? Had her blatant invitation last night disgusted him? Had she been too eager? Good Lord, they weren't exactly children. She might be as inexperienced as someone half her age, but her hormones didn't realize that. Her body was definitely that of a woman in her prime, and living with a man like Ty hadn't helped put out any fires.

Anny heard the jingle of the phone being returned to its cradle, and she tugged the quilt up over her head.

"Anny?"

Silence. Stubborn, go-to-hell silence.

"Anny, I've got to run."

Who's stopping you? I wouldn't dream of trying to slow you down, so move on! Just get the hell out of my house and let me work things out in my own time and in my own way.

"Look, Anny, I'm sorry. Things sort of got out of hand for a few minutes, but no harm done, huh?" He'd come to stand beside the bed, and Anny scrunched down deeper under the mound of covers and willed the floor to give way under his feet.

"That was the lab on the phone. There's a chance we might be able to bring Jennings around without resorting to anti-psychotic drugs. Clifford's been talking to him for the past few hours, and he seems to be responding. He seems to trust us because we're experienced divers, so it looks like I'm elected to take over. Anny? Did you hear me? I'll give you a call when I know what my schedule will be, but I'll definitely be back to pick up a few things before I check into the hotel at Raleigh."

A streak of pale sunlight shafted across the dark wood floor as Ty shifted his weight awkwardly. Finally, he turned and left, closing the door softly behind him. Layers of quilts and blankets had silenced the single strangled cry of dry-eyed pain.

Nine

With a discipline developed over long years of living alone, Anny faced what had to be faced. She'd done it again. Scratch one lover, add another friend.

Not that Ty had been her lover in the real sense of the word. A few near misses didn't exactly constitute a love affair. At least not on his part. As far as she was concerned, the love affair had started long before he'd ever laid a hand on her. Anny knew with painful certainty that it would continue long after he'd moved out of her life. What she'd felt for Sid had been fondness. Ty was a part of her very being.

Shoving the misery into a deep pocket in her heart, she pulled her tan stocking cap over her head and whipped the muffler around her throat. Letting herself out the back door, she turned to the carrier, and then, frowning, looked about. It was gone.

Clutching her arms across her breasts for warmth, Anny crunched her way across the frosted lawn to the shed. Had she finally lost her last marble? She'd planned to move the hawk in its carrier to the mews first thing this morning, and then, after she'd discovered... Could she have buried the hawk and put away the carrier last night without remembering? She'd been under a certain amount of stress, but she didn't think she could have forgotten something like that.

The carrier was on the dusty shelf, where it normally stayed, along with a bundle of tomato stakes, a box of chipped canning jars, and parts from an ancient gasoline-powered generator. A further search produced a shovel with bits of damp earth still clinging to it, and a tiny, fresh grave centered by a single perfect pinecone.

"Oh, Ty," Anny wailed softly, her breath vaporizing in the crisp air. "Why did you have to be so *wonderful*." Not perfect, she conceded silently; far from perfect, but so dear and so wonderful that she'd probably never look at another man.

For several minutes she stood outside in the clear, cold sunshine, filled with a vast sense of emptiness. Then, shoulders heaving in a sigh, she scuffed her way through the dried leaves and leaped up onto the back porch, kicking the mud from her boots before letting herself into the warm kitchen.

After staring morosely at her breakfast for a suitable length of time, Anny got up from the table and looked up the number of her parents' hotel. If she was going to take off for a few days, she'd have to cut short the socializing while they were here.

"But I'd counted on having you for lunch today," Claire protested. "Evan's having lunch at the club with old man Worthington from the bank, and I can't abide his cigars, so I begged off. Now, don't let me down, darling. You know I hate to eat alone. Bakatsias at twelve-thirty, all right?''

Anny spent the morning in the studio, deliberately blocking from her mind everything except the work on the drawing table before her. Only once did she find her concentration slipping. Eyes staring unseeingly at the shadow of her hand as it angled across the surface of the table, she felt the intolerable ache begin deep inside her.

"Oh, Tyrus, why couldn't you have wanted me enough?'' she whispered.

At eleven, she called Persimmon Press and asked for Susan. "Done. All but the frontispiece, and if you can wait another two weeks for that, the rest of the drawings will be on your desk by nine o'clock tomorrow.''

"Who lit a fire under you?''

"I decided to take off for a few days and go to New York with my parents.''

"But I've got your next two assignments all lined up. I put the manuscripts in the mail today. Incidentally, think cover design while you're at it. We lost our design man last week—he went with an advertising firm. Any chance of your moving to Charlotte?''

"Only if my roof falls in, and believe me, that's not too farfetched.''

Anny was ten minutes late for lunch; her mother was twenty. Claire sighed dramatically, shrugging off a white wool serape lined in a silk zebra print, and ordered white wine and black coffee. "I spent the entire morning being drilled in the importance of fiscal responsibility. Deadly!'' She shuddered, and the light that filtered in through the nearby window ruthlessly delineated the fans at the corners of her eyes, the fine lines that rayed out from her glossy Desert Pink lips.

"I didn't think there was anything left to be responsible with," Anny countered. "Wasn't there some sort of trust that turned out to be worthless?"

"Six generations to make it, three to break it. The LeMontroses were nothing if not efficient. Poor old Hannibal was forced to sell off all but that awful old house and the few acres it stood on to pay off his father's debts. The main house was sold a dozen times, at least. Nobody could afford to keep it up. It burned to the ground the year before I met your father, and I cried for a month. I'd never set foot in the place, but it stood for something in Orange County."

Anny sipped her ice water. "I think I must be more Koscienski than LeMontrose."

"According to Evan, there aren't but one or two left, and they're both intensely musical and extremely disagreeable. You're not musical."

Anny covered her smile at the implication. "At least Hannibal was perfectly content where he was. I think he was probably the most profoundly happy man I've ever known." She wasn't interested in family history now. The last thing she needed at this point was a dreary retrospective of what might have been.

"Uncle Hannibal wasn't a typical LeMontrose, and neither are you. I can't imagine either of you ever amassing a fortune, much less gambling one away. Speaking of which, aren't you getting in over your head?"

Over her head? Anny blinked uncertainly. "Financially, you mean?"

"Don't be obtuse, darling. Tyrus Clay strikes me as an extremely dangerous man. How much do you really know about him?"

"Enough to trust him," Anny declared flatly. "And, Mother, we're only friends."

"Famous last words," Claire said dryly. "I've been married to one man for thirty-seven years, but I know more about men in general than you'll ever know. Friendship between a man and a woman is impossible, and you're living together."

"Claire, a few generations ago, women couldn't even vote. Now they're filling some of the highest posts in the nation. Things change, you know."

"Some things never change. I'm serious, Annabelle. Men and women are different. Always were, always will be. A woman can get so wrapped up in a man that she loses her own identity, but a man has his work, and no woman alive can compete with that." She paused to examine a young, attractive woman being seated at a nearby table. Turning back, she sighed. "A man's first and last mistress is his work. It's the real challenge. It's always there, always fresh and new, his own creation. Once I thought that having a baby would change things. It didn't."

Anny caught back the soft sound of distress that rose in her throat. She didn't want to hear this, she really didn't. Yet, it explained so much.

Claire was still talking, bitterness shading the Southern-finishing-school accent. "A woman can spend a fortune on clothes and salons, and it won't make a tad of difference in the long run. There'll always be younger, more beautiful women, and even if he remains technically faithful, there's always his work."

Stunned by the unwelcome revelation, Anny could think of nothing to say. With all her heart she wished the words unspoken, unheard, but it was too late. "Mother..."

"Oh, don't look so tragic," Claire snapped, downing her wine, then sipping her coffee. "If that's the way my little outburst of maternal concern is going to affect you, it's a good thing it doesn't happen too often. I'm going to order something perfectly sinful today, I think. What's that marvelous quiche they do here that's so horribly rich?"

"Oh, I don't know. Describe it to the waiter. He'll know what you mean. Mother—"

"Don't overdo it, darling. 'Claire' will do quite nicely. And I meant what I said about Tyrus. He's entirely too gorgeous and experienced for you. Stick to someone nice and safe, like your schoolteacher friend. Then, when the honeymoon's over, you won't be so utterly destroyed." She squinted at the menu, trailing a rose-tipped, ring-encrusted forefinger down the page. When a handsome young waiter appeared at her side, she smiled up at him beguilingly.

Making aimless circles on a large sheet of newsprint later that afternoon, Anny thought about her mother's words. Could she have misunderstood? Was it possible that all these years she'd been mistaken about her parents? She'd always looked upon their marriage as successful, a sort of closed corporation. With herself an outsider. If she'd been asked to describe their relationship, she'd have called it symbiotic. Claire used her impeccable social contacts to further Evan's career, and

Evan employed his creative flair to finance the life-style that should have been Claire's by right of birth.

"But I'm not Claire," Anny reminded herself firmly. "And Ty is nothing at all like my father."

Crumpling the newsprint and tossing it aside, she taped down a sheet of drawing paper and stared at it, willing an image to take shape. Unlike Claire, she had her own career and her own life to get on with. Thank God for that, at least. She'd never thought of Claire as particularly strong; she was simply Claire—beautiful, even kind in an abstract sort of way, her style undiminished by age.

She was stronger than she looked, Anny realized now. But Anny was strong, too. Anny had lived alone far too long ever to be totally dependent on any man. If she couldn't have Tyrus—and she couldn't—then she'd survive without him. The joy might go out of living for a while, but at least she knew how to put one foot in front of the other and keep moving until the worst of the hurting was over.

She was still working some seven hours later when Ty called. Rolling her neck to relieve the tension such close work engendered, she reached for the phone.

"Anny? Ty. Listen, I stopped by at noon and picked up a few things. Looks like I'll be here at the lab until all hours, and after that I'll be going directly to Raleigh. Cass is getting in ahead of schedule, so I won't be out to the house for a while. Got a pencil? Jot down this number in case you need to reach me. It's the hotel's."

Anny stared stonily at the row of framed drawings on the wall, not bothering to write down the number. It would be a cold day in hell before she needed to get in touch with him.

"Anny? Got that? Listen, are you sure you're all right?"

"Of course I'm all right. Why wouldn't I be all right?" Relenting, she added, "Ty, thanks for doing the hawk for me. I really appreciate it."

He started to speak, but she cut him off. If she softened now, she was lost. "As a matter of fact, I'm glad you called. I'll be going to New York with Claire and Evan, after all. Claire's right, I am in a rut. It's been years since I've been anywhere exciting. You have your key, so make yourself at home."

This time the silence was on Ty's part. Anny's fingers, slippery with sudden moisture, squeezed the receiver until they actually hurt. She felt a physical hunger to reach out to him. "Ty? Do me one more favor?"

A pause, then Ty's gruff voice said, "Sure, Anny, you name it."

Fighting against the urge to plead with him to forget Cass and come home where he belonged, she forced herself to speak calmly. "If we have a hard rain, will you check on the buckets in the attic? They freeze and split on the bottom sometimes, and it causes an awful mess when they thaw out."

"What about the outside faucets?"

"The outside faucets. Well, the one outside the kitchen works, but the one under the dining room window— that's sort of the library, remember? It froze ages ago and I never had it fixed, and the one on the front—oh, forget it." Suddenly she was sick of the responsibility of the ancient, decrepit house, sick of Tyrus and his conscientious concern, sick of everything. "Look, just forget it. It's not that vital, and you've got more important things to do than nurse my plumbing problems."

Hanging up the phone with no more than a curt good-bye, Anny leaned against the wall and covered her face with one arm. *And if you bring that—that* woman *out here to my house, you're in deep trouble*, she vowed silently. And she'd know. Her intuition would tell her the minute she walked through the door if Ty and Cass had made love in her house, in that brass bed upstairs, while she'd been in New York with her parents.

"Look, Cass, I'm sorry. I saw a chance to grab a few hours of sleep and I took it. You know damned well if I'd gone to the hotel, sleep's the last thing I'd be getting." Raking furrows through his hair, Ty held the phone away from his ear until the fireworks on the other end abated. He'd left himself wide open for that one. So far, they hadn't managed more than a quick dinner and a few minutes snatched between her clients' interviews and Ty's shifts in the lab. Now he'd had to put her off again, and he'd called to explain. "I *know* what I promised! That doesn't mean I've got nothing to do but—"

In growing exasperation, he listened to the shrill voice on the other end. When she paused for a breath, he tried again. "Cass, the dive isn't over just because they've started decompression, and— No, dammit! There's no way I can drive to Raleigh now. I got four hours' sleep out of the past thirty-six, and I don't care if the governor is going to dance on the damned flagpole. I am not going to any gubernatorial *function*!"

His patience strained long past the breaking point, he tried to be fair. After all, he'd half promised...

"Tyrus," Cass argued, "this is not just another Elvis impersonator. This time I'm selling solid talent. My client is going straight to the top, and I'm the one who set it up.

He'd still be priming tobacco and singing in the church choir if I hadn't used my contacts to get him into the festival. He's going to perform for the governor, the Cultural Resources people, and half the money on the eastern seaboard. Now, are you telling me that you can't take a few measly hours off for the biggest catch of my career? This is important to me, Tyrus. Don't you even care?''

"Cass—honey, you don't need me there. Hell, I don't even own a tux."

"So go out and rent one."

"Cass, I'd fall asleep in the soup." The truth was, he'd never been able to fit into anything that wasn't tailored expressly to allow for his diver's chest and his swimmer's shoulders.

The husky voice took on a seductive quality as Cass switched her tactics. "I know where there's a king-sized bed going to waste. If I'd known you weren't going to be sharing it with me, I'd have booked into Howard Johnson's along with the rest of the crew."

Massaging the back of his neck, Ty grimaced. What could he say? He'd had every intention of checking into the hotel the day Cass arrived, only how was he to know the dive would be at a critical stage? "Honey, I'm sorry as I can be, but—"

"You *talk* a good game," Cass said pointedly. "What's wrong? Afraid you still can't deliver?"

He could feel the familiar tightness gathering at the base of his skull, the familiar pounding at his temples. "How much longer will you be in town? Do you have to stick with your protégé until you get him safely back home?"

"I could probably stay over another day or so, but why should I bother? You're still making excuses. As far as I can see, nothing's changed."

The implication was obvious, and in tired desperation, Ty ran over the situation in his mind. While his presence wasn't actually required at the lab, after years of conditioning he couldn't get over the feeling of responsibility for any diver in trouble.

Poor Jennings. He was every bit as distant as if he were half a mile deep under mountainous seas instead of inside a shore-based laboratory surrounded by banks of experts. What that poor devil was undergoing now could help other divers survive, but that didn't make his personal hell any easier to endure. And reasonable or not, Ty felt obligated to be there. He'd been on the threshold of that same brand of hell once, and it had taken the last shred of control he possessed just to hang on and keep the kid from going over the edge.

Massaging the back of his neck, he sighed. "Look, can I get back to you, Cass? I'll do my best. I'll know by tomorrow morning whether or not I can make it, but either way, I'll be in touch, okay? If I can't make the dinner, I'll try to meet you afterward."

He hung up the phone, swore softly under his breath, and wished it was daylight so that he could go outside and split a cord or two of wood. The trouble with his current situation was that it engendered far more frustrations than it burned up. He needed someone right now to talk him down so he could get a few hours of sleep.

He needed a drink. He needed a lot of drinks! Instead, he made himself a dose of strong black tea. Adding a generous amount of milk, he lifted his mug in a mocking toast.

"Women," he muttered.

After a long moment of brutal self-examination, Ty admitted to himself that what he was undergoing at ground level, with all the air in the world to breathe, wasn't so far removed from sheer panic. Had it been building unconsciously from the moment Cass had called to say she'd arrived in Raleigh? Hell, that was crazy! It just didn't make sense. Wasn't this what he'd been working toward ever since he'd left Wilmington? A chance to get himself on track again and get back to their old relationship? So how come now that everything was working for him, he was shying away?

Scared of laying it on the line, old boy? Scared of making a fool of yourself one more time? Scared of being laughed out of the bedroom?

Expelling a heavy sigh, he sipped the lukewarm tea, wishing it were good whiskey. That witch had gotten him so damned health conscious that he hadn't had a decent drink in over a month.

She'd been good for him in all other ways, too. He'd been going downhill fast, like a chunk of rusty machinery, when she'd jerked him up out of his self-pity and made him take a good look at what he was jeopardizing.

So where was she? Some friend she'd turned out to be! Why wasn't she back here, where she belonged? He needed to talk to her, needed the feeling of confidence she gave him, the feeling of...

He didn't know what the devil he needed from her. All he knew was that these few weeks of living with her had brought him a feeling of...peace. No, peace wasn't quite the word; it didn't describe the sense of excitement living with a woman like Anny gave him. Just lately he'd

begun to wake up each morning with a feeling of anticipation, as if a new day in itself was enough of a miracle.

"Cripes, now she's got me thinking like one of those
damned philosophy books of hers!"

Yet, Ty acknowledged grudgingly, hadn't he been
aware of a sense of incompleteness all these years, as
though he were missing out on something important? So
maybe he didn't know all the answers. Maybe he never
would, but at least that nagging feeling was gone.

It had been a hasty act, her decision to go to New
York. In the days that followed, Anny had had more than
enough time to repent. Yet, it hadn't been all bad. She'd
seen little of Evan during the days. He was either on the
phone or on the run, making appointments, renewing
contacts, hard-nosed by day, then charming, if slightly
distracted, by night. Anny tried to see her father through
Claire's eyes. She soon gave it up as irrelevant. He was
simply a man who'd designed a future for himself and
then set about making it happen, using a knowledge of
textiles and a flair for fashion as a cornerstone. She could
admire his success in some areas, not in others.

Claire at fifty-eight was still beautiful, but it took
longer each year for her to achieve her particular style of
beauty, longer at the end of each day to recover. For the
first time, Anny was allowed to see her mother *au natu-
rel*—face mask, foot soak, bifocals, and all.

The shopping spree was held to a minimum at Anny's
insistence. Also at her insistence, the money she spent
was her own. The roof had waited this long; it could wait
another year.

By the evening of the fourth day, she could stand it no
longer. Nothing had changed. The ache was still there,

that raw feeling of loss and anger and helplessness. Dammit, he *needed* her! If they hadn't been meant for each other, why had fate dumped him on her doorstep to turn her whole life upside down?

She called the airport, argued, insisted, and cajoled. And then she crammed her belongings, new and old, into a single suitcase, placating Claire while she pushed back the doubts that rose to haunt her. Would he still be at the hotel in Raleigh with Cass, or would he be waiting at home when Anny got there?

Either way, she had to pull herself together and get on with the rest of her life. She promised Evan to have her hair styled, promised Claire to write often, promised herself to be a better daughter, and tipped the doorman two dollars for handing her small suitcase into the cab.

Oh, Lord, she hated herself in this mood!

Damn her, what was she trying to pull? Ty paced the cluttered room, scowling at every evidence of Anny's particular bent as a decorator. Shoes by the front door, shoes by the back door, the pair under the coffee table. No wonder her feet were always cold. There were books everywhere, not to mention those jars of dried weeds and the scraps of rusty metal. On a dusty mahogany table sat a beautiful china bowl filled with arrowheads and corroded shell fragments that dated back to the Civil War. An interest in history, hell, the woman was a natural-born pack rat! Or an out-and-out adventurer.

The twist of his lips was more a grimace than an actual smile. Who was he to call someone else an adventurer? He'd yet to meet a diver who didn't have the heart of an adventurer. Some of them outgrew it; most never did.

The grimace faded, and his eyes assumed the bleakness that had seldom been absent for the past four days. Between Anny and Jennings, they'd managed to ruin his whole reunion with Cass. What was supposed to have been a triumphant occasion had been reduced to a fiasco. Not once had he managed to spend a single night with her, and even when they'd gotten together for dinner, he'd been too tired and she'd been too keyed up. They'd ended up on the verge of another squabble. She'd gotten a call from a TV talk-show host and spent fifteen minutes scheduling a taping while her lobster congealed in its butter. Ty had left soon after that, already regretting his dietary lapse.

He had half a mind to walk out of here, freeze or no freeze, and let the damned pipes burst. He'd emptied the buckets in the attic and checked the outside of the house, wrapping faucets and draining hoses. The place was falling apart. Oh, it was attractive enough, with its wide planks and its intricate millwork, but it needed far more attention than she was willing or able to give it.

Too busy looking after hawks. Too busy traipsing around the countryside digging up scrap metal and watching beavers dam up a river. Or running off to New York.

And what the hell did he care, anyway? Let her party all night with all the fun people. "The fun people," he jeered. Was that all women wanted? First Cass, and now Anny? Didn't they have any appreciation for the *real* things in life?

He'd give his right arm for a stiff drink, but he felt guilty enough without that. Since Cass had been in town, his diet had gone down the drain. Cass liked rich, heavily seasoned foods, and somehow it hadn't seemed to matter anymore. It had been a complete washout from start to finish, his grand reunion. He'd missed the big function, despite the best of intentions, and she'd been furious.

"You've never done a single thing I wanted to do," she'd accused when she'd finally turned up at the hotel at a quarter of two in the morning. He'd gone there directly from the lab, dead tired and in no mood to hassle, and then had to cool his heels in the lobby until she'd come in. She'd finally shown up, looking like a spangled butterfly and smelling of bourbon and the heavy, exotic perfume she always wore.

"Honey, I told you why I couldn't go with you tonight," he'd explained patiently. They'd gone up to her room, and Ty had glanced longingly at the bed, stifling a yawn. What with putting in so many nights at the lab, he was beginning to lose track of day and night.

"Oh, sure, you and your precious work! If it's not some floating old rust bucket or one of those stinking, cigar-chewing cronies of yours, it's some make-work project cooked up to make ex-divers like you feel important!"

The pulse at his temple had started up again; it seemed to go hand in hand with clenched fists and a sour feeling in his stomach. "It's slightly more than that," he'd insisted. "In case you weren't aware of it, we're living on a planet of water, and it's getting pretty damned crowded. The sea bed has enough in the way of resources—foods, minerals, fuels—to make the difference between—"

"Oh, get off your soapbox. What was I supposed to do for a dinner partner? All day I waited for you to call, and when I tried to reach you at work I was told by some jerk that you couldn't come to the phone. *Couldn't come to the phone*," she repeated, each word dripping with disbelief.

"Cass, if there'd been any way I could have gone to that party with you tonight, I'd have done it. I've counted the days until I'd see you again, don't you know that?"

Had he? Or had he stopped counting somewhere along the line?

"Oh, sure you have," she snarled disbelievingly, the pointed toe of her silver sandal rapping out a silent tattoo on the carpet. "What if I hadn't come to Raleigh?"

"I'd have gone back to Wilmington as soon as I was free."

"Really?" Patches of angry color marred the careful pattern of her blusher, and Ty managed to hang on to his temper by a thread.

Feet braced apart, he took a deep breath and reminded himself that this was the woman who'd sent him into a tailspin not too long ago. "Really," he echoed, his voice deceptively calm. "Cass, I've been thinking of buying a small trawler and a place somewhere near the water. My plans were to be back on the coast by the first of the year, one way or another."

"A trawler! You mean you're going to be a commercial fisherman?"

There was no pleasing a woman. To hell with it! He'd reached for her then, pulling her against him and walking her toward the bed. "Don't worry, there'll be more than enough time for us," he'd said in one last attempt to placate her. They'd never been able to talk. The only place they'd ever been able to communicate had been in bed.

That was when things had really started falling apart. Remembering, Ty swore relentlessly. Cass had thawed out with the first kiss. The trouble was, the more she thawed, the more he froze. Her hands were everywhere, but at that point, instead of taking the offensive as he'd always done in the past, he'd found himself acting like some scared virgin, fighting to keep his pants on.

Desperately, he'd done his best to distract her. "Mmm, what's the name of that perfume you're wearing?" His clothes would reek of it for hours. Unbidden, he'd recalled the subtle wildflower scent that Anny wore, and turned his head aside.

Insinuating one of her legs between his, Cass had whispered a word in his ear—a word, like the perfume, designed to arouse.

The trouble was, it had had the opposite effect. He'd been completely turned off. By the time he'd managed to get himself disengaged, he'd accepted the fact that he'd never even been turned on.

It hadn't been a case of outright failure this time, no matter what Cass had accused him of. And furious, she'd thrown them all at him, the ugly terms, the unflattering descriptions. He'd been lucky to get out in one piece. Racing home along an empty highway, he'd checked himself over for damage and found surprisingly little. Miraculously, his sense of masculinity had come away without a scratch.

There'd be no going back after this. Wherever he and Cass were headed from here on out, it surely wouldn't be together. He had nothing to offer a woman like Cass, and God knows, she had nothing he wanted. The amazing thing was that it had lasted as long as it had. How blind could a man be without even realizing it?

"Where the devil *is* that woman?" Ty demanded once more of the empty house. "How long does it take to buy a new coat, for God's sake?"

Parties. Claire had said there'd be parties, that all the best people would be there. Who in blazes were "all the best people," anyway? Anny's list and her parents' wouldn't include many of the same names; he'd stake his life on that. After seeing her against the background of her parents, Ty understood a lot of things about Anny. And if there was one thing she had squared away, it was a solid set of values.

He wished to God she and her values would come home. Morosely, Ty stared at the empty fireplace. It was drafty in here, but it hardly seemed worthwhile to build a fire for one person.

The first day after Anny had left, he'd come back here after a marathon session with Jennings and canceled his plans to check into the hotel. Jennings, poor devil, was holding his own now, and they hadn't had to administer the anti-psychotic drugs after all. It had been touch-and-go for a while, and Ty had been exhausted. The house had been cold and empty, but he'd switched on the electric blanket and crashed for ten hours straight.

Since then, juggling Cass and his work, he'd fallen behind on his sleep again, but it wasn't sleep he needed now. Restlessly, he moved through the empty rooms, seeing her personality everywhere. Who but Anny would get such a kick out of digging up a few worthless old relics?

He wandered up to her studio and opened the door, and it was like stepping into another world. Spacious, orderly, clean, it had been painted off-white—floor, walls, and ceiling. There were three large windows that had obviously been added recently, and two large drawing tables, one flat, one slanted. Supplies were kept in meticulous order on open shelves, and half a dozen businesslike lamps stood ready to illuminate the tables and the desk that took up space in one corner.

Ty entered the room, surprised to discover that he felt her presence in these austere surroundings as much as he did in the cluttered rooms downstairs. A line of framed drawings hung in a single row along one wall. He studied them, instinctively recognizing the quality of the work. There was a series of landscapes, two or three portraits, but most were nature studies, cross-sections of plants, close-ups of flowers, leaves, and seeds.

Several of the landscapes looked familiar to him. Wasn't that the group of rocks where they'd picnicked that day she'd walked his feet off? There was a whole collection of bird drawings. Those hideous creatures with the bulbous eyes must be young owls; the ones with all the gaping beaks, her hand-raised babies.

She was good, she was very good. Her work reflected none of the clutter or the disorganization he'd have expected from her. There was a quality and a style that set her drawings apart, lending them a certain elegance that even he could recognize.

She was good, all right. And she was gone.

And he wanted her to be here. He *needed* her to be here.

Ten

It was late, and Anny had never liked driving at night. She'd been unable to get a direct flight on such short notice, and the crowded flight she'd boarded had been delayed on takeoff for almost forty-five minutes. After running for what seemed like miles through the airport in Washington, she'd changed planes with mere minutes to spare. Her baggage had not been so fortunate.

So much for her shopping spree. Two new dresses and a sixty-dollar sweater were on their way to points unknown, her coat had been crushed under three attaché cases in the overhead compartment. Meanwhile, the world's worst hot dog had dribbled mustard on her new silk blouse, she'd snagged her gray designer hose, and the gray lizard shoes Evan had insisted she buy had crippled her for life.

Home. There was a lot to be said for just being there, be it ever so cold and empty. As soon as she got in, she'd build a roaring fire, get into her pajamas and bathrobe, make herself a giant pot of strong tea, and curl up on the couch. Maybe she'd even sleep there, just for tonight.

But if she did, it would only be because it was warmer than her bedroom, not because her bed was haunted by a memory of what had almost happened there. She couldn't afford to get bogged down in sentimentality; she had the rest of her life to get on with.

Headlights tunneled through the darkness, picking out familiar landmarks: a dead sycamore, a narrow bridge, the lights of her nearest neighbor. Anny's gloved fingers gripped the wheel and she wrenched her mind away from dangerous channels and back onto the work still to be done on the O'Hara book. She'd get on that frontispiece first thing tomorrow, and the minute it was finished she'd tackle the next project. No. First she'd go to the post office and collect her mail, and then, as soon as the frontispiece was done, she'd be all set to start reading the new manuscripts and planning the illustrations. No time to think.

"This time I'll reward myself, I really will," she promised faithfully as she turned off the pavement onto the graveled road. Hannibal had always given her some small reward at the completion of every project—a book of poems, a bouquet, a bottle of her favorite wine. She'd fully intended to carry on the tradition, only as often as not, she forgot. This time she wouldn't forget. "An overhead projector, and the roof can wait another few months," she decided, forgetting for the moment that her roof fund had been wiped out again by her shopping binge.

The lights were on, and Anny sagged. She hadn't dared let herself hope. Pulling up beside the house, she switched off the engine and sat there. What now? Play it cool? Toss off a casual greeting, as though she hadn't spent every waking hour thinking about him, every sleeping one dreaming of him? Was she really capable of overlooking the fact that he'd climbed out of her warm bed and gone directly to Cass?

And what if he wasn't alone? If Cass was with him, what then?

The front door opened, and Ty's rangy silhouette blocked the light for an instant. And then he was beside the car, yanking open her door, scowling down at her as he reached around to undo her seatbelt.

"Well? What the devil are you waiting for, an engraved invitation? Are you alone?"

"No, I've got the whole blasted Patagonian Philharmonic Orchestra crammed into the backseat," she shot back, scrabbling around for her purse and the spy novel she'd bought in the airport and would probably never get around to reading.

"I see you had a great vacation," Ty said sarcastically, ushering her inside and slamming the door. He'd gone out in his shirt sleeves, and now he blew on his fingers, glaring at her as though she were an intruder. "What's the matter, too many parties? Too many late hours with all those *fun people*?"

Desperately tired, Anny dropped her purse on a chair and shed her coat. At least the house was warm, even if her welcome wasn't. "Tyrus?" She shot him a level look. "Will you shut up?"

"You look like the very devil."

"And you're your old sweet self again, I see." At least Cass was nowhere in sight. Of course, she might be hiding upstairs; at this point, Anny's intuition was too tired to function. "What's the matter, did your playmate get tired of your nasty disposition and walk out on you again? I can't say I blame her."

"Why didn't you let me know when you were coming home?"

"Why? So you could get rid of any incriminating evidence? It is my home, in case you've forgotten."

"I haven't forgotten a blasted thing! Where's your luggage?"

"By now it's probably in Cincinnati! Stop yelling at me, Tyrus." Anny stepped out of her shoes and kicked them aside.

"I am not yelling at you," he barked. "I am trying to be helpful, but you're not making it easy!"

"Go help Cass. I don't need your help!" *Oh, you fool! Why don't you just get a green neon sign and spell it out for him?*

Anny turned blindly toward her bedroom, intent only on escaping before she destroyed the few shreds of pride she had left. What on earth was happening to her? She'd planned to play it so cool, but before she'd even said hello, she was screeching out wild accusations about a woman she'd never even met. Any man with half a brain would know she was sizzling with jealousy.

But if he'd had the nerve to bring that woman here, she thought, yanking viciously on her doorknob... She shook her head. "It's none of my business. I don't want to know about it," she muttered under her breath.

"Anny, you're tired." His tone of voice struck her as unbearably condescending, and the temper

she'd been struggling to harness broke the bonds once
more.

"I am *not* tired, and don't you tell me I *am*! Dammit,
I don't need this, Tyrus. If you've brought her home with
you, then that's your affair. The room is yours. There's
nothing in your lease that says you can't invite a guest to
share it, but don't play games with me. I'm not in the
mood."

She was inside her room, her angry breath clearly visible in the icy air, when he caught her by the arm and
swung her around. Anny looked pointedly at the hand on
her arm and then up past the formidable chin—a chin
that looked as though it hadn't been shaven in days.

She met the steely glint of his eyes head on, and her lips
tightened ominously. One more word would release the
whole logjam, and she had too much pride to let him
know how much she was hurting. Head tilted at an im-
possibly arrogant angle, she waited until he released her
arm.

"Anny, we need to talk." Drawing her outside, Ty
closed the door.

"I don't think so," she said dismissively, opening the
door again. Maybe she'd simply hibernate. Maybe she'd
come out again next spring, when all danger of a killing
frost was past. Maybe she wasn't as resilient as she'd
thought.

"Don't go."

Her hand on the cold china knob, Anny hesitated.
Without looking up, she said, "Ty, I'm beat. It's been an
exhausting four days, I had a lousy trip back, they lost
my luggage, these shoes have ruined my feet, and—"

"Anny, I've missed you."

She shot him an openly skeptical look. "I doubt that," she said flatly, her shoulders braced in an unconscious attitude of defense. "Between Cass and the lab, I doubt that you had much time to miss anything."

"I didn't spend a lot of time at the hotel," Ty said quietly. "There were some developments with the dive, and then two of the technicians monitoring it came down with the flu and the rest of us had to work double shifts."

"Rotten luck. I hope you and Cass managed to spend some time together." She hoped nothing of the kind. She hoped that Cass Valenti had sprouted warts and flown away on a broomstick.

"I could make tea," Ty offered hopefully, and closing her eyes to the voice of common sense, Anny let her shoulders sag in surrender.

"That sounds marvelous," she confessed. "The pan for warming the milk is hanging inside the pantry door."

"Warm the milk," Ty repeated, turning toward the kitchen and then veering back to the fireplace. "I'll just build up the fire so I can warm the honey on the hearth. No ants."

Anny leaned her forehead against the cool paneled door for just a moment, the smile on her face hidden from view. Oh, God, she loved this man. There didn't seem to be much future in it, even if Cass was no longer a threat. And she couldn't even be certain of that much. All she had to go on was that erratic intuition of hers telling her that Cass was out of the picture.

Of course, she reminded herself conscientiously, that could very well be wishful thinking. Besides, any man who'd managed to stay single for thirty-eight years obviously wasn't looking very hard for a wife, and Anny was afraid she couldn't handle anything less than a lifetime commitment. Whoever said it was better to have loved and lost probably hadn't.

"Give me ten minutes," she called over her shoulder. She felt grimy from the trip. Shedding her clothes as she headed for the shower, she wished fervently that her luggage had come home with her. Claire had presented her with a perfectly frivolous nightgown ensemble after seeing the flannel pajamas and serviceable bathrobe Anny had taken to New York.

"Good heaven, you can't order a room-service breakfast in those rags," she'd declared, horrified.

Slinging soapsuds wildly, Anny hummed snatches of a show tune she'd heard a few nights before. It was a love song, the old-fashioned kind that never quite went out of style. She patted herself dry, slicked on a handful of lotion, threw talc over both shoulders, and tossed the can aside before climbing into another pair of flannel pajamas and brushing her hair. A soak in the tub would have helped ease some of the travel weariness from her bones, but there wasn't time. Come to think of it, she wasn't quite as tired as she'd thought. Leaning toward the steamy mirror, her face melted into a broad smile.

"One of those old wooden tubs would be perfect, wouldn't it?" she said by way of greeting when she returned to the living room and backed up to the blazing fire. If Ty weren't there, she'd have flipped up her shirt, dropped her britches, and let the fire warm her naked backside. Nothing better on a cold night.

"For bathing before the fire, you mean? I'm not sure I'd fit."

With his gaze moving over her, dwelling on the camouflaged curves of her breasts and hips, Anny wished she'd taken time to dig out Hannibal's old bathrobe. The white flannel garment she'd thought so modest suddenly seemed extraordinarily revealing. "Maybe we could get a hogshead from one of the tobacco companies around here," she teased, fingering the top button in an uncharacteristic gesture of nervousness. "That's about your size."

"I think a standard hot tub would fill the bill," Ty said with a grin, placing a steaming mug of milky tea on the coffee table and handing her the honey container.

"Far too decadent for this neck of the woods." Anny shook her head, catching a stream of golden sourwood honey and licking it from her finger. "A sauna; now, that's different. Did you know that the American Indians were using saunas hundreds of years ago? Lends them a certain distinction, doesn't it?"

Settling himself at the other end of the couch, Ty extended his legs under the coffee table without encountering any foreign objects for once. "Distinction or not, I could have used one these past few days."

"I'm not sure they're recommended for people with hypertension, but you could ask. How's the diet? Have you had time to do any exercising? I suppose you've been too busy."

Tell her, Ty exhorted himself silently. *She just handed you the perfect opening, so tell her what shape you were in when you got here and how far you've come, thanks to her and an understanding medic.*

"It'll have to wait, anyway. I just shot my roof fund on a bundle of new clothes I'll probably never wear again." Anny sipped her tea, not particularly concerned over the fact that her budget was ruined and her house was gradually disintegrating, and she could hardly afford a birdbath, much less a sauna or a hot tub. It was really rather alarming to realize how little it took to make her truly happy: a pot of tea, a roaring fire, and thou. But mostly thou, she admitted freely.

Ty was staring at a shower of sparks in one corner of the fireplace, and she allowed her gaze to roam over him, taking in the swell of his chest, the shadow of his beard. He did look tired. There were deep lines grooving his lean cheeks, lines that hadn't been there before. "Has it been rough?" she asked softly.

"Rough enough." Ty nodded. "Jennings is out of the woods now, but it'll still be a long haul. The thing with Cass was a washout."

They weren't touching, and yet it seemed as if they'd never been so close. But if he was waiting for a word of sympathy on that score, he was out of luck. Anny did the next best thing. "Are you sorry?"

"Relieved." Ty placed his mug on top of a stack of papers he'd brought home with him and turned to face her. Cass was a million miles away. It was as though she'd never existed. The important thing was Anny. If he loused this up...

God, he was shaking like a leaf! Where did he begin? Should he risk scaring her off with a declaration, or should he pave the way with a medical history and a summary of his immediate prospects? In the endless hours while he'd been waiting for her to come home, he'd rehearsed several possible openings, but for the life of him, he couldn't remember a single one.

Raking an unsteady hand through his hair, he blurted out, "Anny, I've missed you, but I need a shower, a shave, and about ten hours of sleep before I can do much about it. Will you wait for me?" *Coward, coward!*

Anny didn't know whether to laugh or cry. He'd missed her, but he was too tired and sleepy to do anything about it. She shrugged. "I'll be around."

"If it's not too much to ask, could I use your shower? The knob came off the heat register in the bathroom upstairs, and I haven't had time to fix it."

"Be my guest. Oh, wait!" Scrambling up, she hurried out with some excuse about towels. She'd been so anxious to get back to him that she'd left the bathroom littered with clothes, towels, dusting powder, and Lord only knew what else. It was probably too late, but she would like to make a decent impression on him. Her intuition was hammering out messages again, messages she didn't dare allow herself to believe. Still, there was always a chance that it was right.

When she got back, Ty was sound asleep. Face crumpling in dismay, Anny sank down on a chair and studied his limp form. He had on the canvas deck shoes he wore around the house, and a pair of worn jeans that lovingly encased his hard, muscular body. His blue flannel shirt was open several buttons deep at the throat, and he was completely irresistible: rumpled hair, lined face, stubbled chin, and all.

Quietly, Anny eased the shoes from his feet and swung his legs onto the couch. He never stirred. When one of his arms fell to the floor, she picked it up and laid it across his waist, marveling at how heavy the human arm was. Then she covered him with an afghan.

For a long time, she stood over him, her eyes following the complex curves of his mouth and the sun-bleached tips of his lashes as they splayed out over sharply hewn cheekbones. The color of flint, those eyes of his, but she'd seen them as dark as obsidian, the pupils all but covering the iris. With any luck at all, she would again.

It was the draft that aroused her sometime during the night, and for just an instant Anny had trouble remembering where she was. Still at the Berkshire Palace? Back in her own bed?

She was on the floor in the living room, on a pile of quilts, covered with still more. Right where she'd fallen asleep. The draft had been caused by someone's lifting the top layer of covers.

"Shh!" Ty whispered. "Go back to sleep."

Her heart slammed against her rib cage as her pulse went into overdrive. Go back to sleep? With that solid wall of masculine warmth lowering down beside her? He gathered her into his arms just as he'd done that other time. Only this time Anny was wide awake. This time she wouldn't be taken by surprise.

"Ty, what are you doing here?" she whispered, as the clean, soapy scent of him filled her nostrils.

"I told you we needed to talk."

"You told me you needed a shower, a shave, and ten hours of sleep," she corrected, finding an obscure sense of safety in minutiae. She was trembling, every muscle in her body clenched.

"I had the last first, and the first last. That was after I woke up to find myself all tucked in and you bedded down beside me on the floor." He'd already discovered the buttons of her shirt and was making short work of releasing them. He'd told her once that he'd developed eyes in his fingertips by doing underwater repairs at zero degrees visibility.

"My bedroom was frigid. I thought I might as well take advantage of the fire," she rationalized. *Last chance to go ashore,* a voice warned silently.

"It had almost gone out. I put on another log before I showered. Do you always keep your talc in the soap dish?"

"I was in a hurry."

"So am I," Ty whispered as his lips brushed aside her hair to caress the hidden warmth of her nape. "So am I."

I thought we were going to talk. Whatever happened to talking? The thought glinted through her mind like a reflection on sunlit water, and was as quickly lost.

He turned her in his arms, and for the first time Anny discovered that he had nothing on. "Ty," she said, instincts and urges at war within her, "is this going to be another near miss? I mean, if you're just trying to be friendly—"

The rest of her warning was lost as his hands slipped under the waistband of her pajamas and cupped the cool firmness of her flesh. His eyes, in the dim glow of firelight, were dark, gleaming slits. To Anny's amazement, he was trembling even more than she was.

"I'm going to be extremely friendly," Ty declared. "Let's get you out of these clothes." He eased off her cumbersome pajama shirt and tossed it aside, holding her away from him. Firelight turned the pale cones of her breasts into glowing coral, and he released his breath in a long, shuddering sigh. "So lovely...so incredibly beautiful."

He caught her to him then. Crushed against the wiry dark hair on his deep chest, Anny felt her nipples tighten into hard, throbbing knots. She fought down the sudden rise of panic. It was as though she'd stepped aboard a racing roller coaster with no time to fasten her safety belt.

"Ty?" The small sound was a plea for reassurance, but it was too late. For better or worse, she was already being swept along. There was no getting off, no turning back.

When the tip of his tongue swirled around one rosy areola, she moaned and twisted to bring the other breast to his attention. Her hands were busy on a feverish mission of their own, discovering a world of exciting textures, of satin and fur, of velvet-sheathed steel.

"Oh, sweetheart, we've got to slow down—I can't take much more." The taut words grated against the sounds of ragged breathing, and then his hands were slipping under her shoulders, moving down her back. Cupping the swell of her buttocks in his palms, he lifted her hips, and she felt the earth dip and waver at the force of his driving arousal.

Lightning streaked through her, fueling fires already burning out of control, setting off alarms that clamored unheeded. With an instinct born of sheer need, her hands began to play over his body. Even before the last fragment of caution broke off and drifted away unnoticed, she was beginning to discover new ways to touch, new ways to kiss.

Moving abruptly, Ty positioned himself over her, a sheen of perspiration covering his flushed face. His eyes were narrowed, almost as if he were in pain. "Anny, I can't wait any longer," he grated harshly. "I've never wanted anything so much in all my life!"

Shaken with the intensity of a matching need, Anny cradled him eagerly in the heated embrace of her thighs. There was no thought in her heart of denying him. She

was his. Didn't he know? Hadn't they both been hur-
tling through eons of time and space toward this very
moment?

With a strength that bordered on ruthlessness, Ty took
her. Mere seconds later, a guttural cry broke from his
lips. Drenched in sweat, he collapsed, rolling onto his side
and taking her with him.

"Anny, Anny," he whispered hoarsely, "you don't
know what you've done for me."

Dejectedly, Anny sank back to earth. One minute she'd
been soaring to cosmic heights; the next, she'd been
watching a comet spin past, knowing it was far too late
for her to match its orbit. She was back where she started,
flat on the ground.

And you didn't even bother to kiss me, she accused silently, resenting the ragged sound of his breathing beside her. She stared over his shoulder into the graying
dawn, wondering what had gone wrong. Had she expected too much? Probably. It wouldn't be the first time
she'd set her hopes on a shooting star and had to settle for
a falling leaf.

So much for dreams and expectations. It was probably her fault, anyway. A long, tepid engagement not-
withstanding, she was about as inexperienced as a woman
could be. Sid had not been particularly physical, and
she'd never found the game worth the bother.

Fighting against a feeling of overwhelming letdown,
Anny eyed the distance to the bathroom door. She could
make a run for it and lock herself in until after he'd left
for work. Maybe by the time they met again, she'd be
able to face him and pretend that nothing had happened.

That was it; she'd simply ignore it. And if Ty was crass
enough to refer to what had happened, she'd look him

directly in the eye and lie through her teeth. "You made *love* to me?" she'd ask. "I really haven't the foggiest notion what you're talking about. You must have been dreaming."

And she must have been dreaming to think anything had changed while she was gone. So he'd quarreled with Cass again and now he'd taken out his frustrations on her, and she was still enough of a fool to be head-over-heels in love with the wretch.

"Anny, I'm sorry." The soft rasp of his words tightened her resolution, and she remained perfectly still, pretending to be asleep.

"Anny? Don't hide from me, sweetheart."

Sweetheart? *Sweetheart?* What was he up to now? Not content to raid her body, he had to have her heart and soul as well?

She felt his lips brush her forehead, and she clamped her eyes tightly shut, aware that she was being unreasonable. But what else could she do? She had so few defenses where he was concerned, and he kept battering them down, if not with simple kindness, by creating needs within her that he was evidently either unwilling or incapable of fulfilling.

Still pretending to be asleep, she flopped over on her side, only to have him pull her back. "Anny! Dammit, Anny! Open your eyes and look at me!" His arms held her tightly, and one of his thighs slid over hers, preventing her from escaping.

"Would you *mind*?" she demanded fiercely.

As though she hadn't even protested, as though she was still as eager and as pliable as she'd been a few minutes before instead of stiff and resistant, Ty smiled down at her. "Anny, you've just made me the happiest man in the world. It's only fair to try and return the favor."

"Forget it," she said bitingly. "I already have."

"Never. Can't stand being in debt. Now hush up and listen to me for just a minute, will you? It's important."

She'd spare him one minute. "Talk fast," she warned.

Amusement warred with some less easily identifiable element as Ty took in the belligerent set of her jaw, the thrust of her bottom lip. He'd been a selfish jerk. And a blind one. The least he could have done was explain first, but somehow, every time he got near her, all his plans went up in smoke. So now he'd gone off like a four-alarm fire, and she'd been disappointed, and that wouldn't do much for his bargaining position.

Ty was still struggling for a way to explain why he'd lost control when Anny pulled away and climbed out of the tangle of bedclothes. Standing over him, completely nude and every bit as regal as the grandest duchess, she glared down her nose at him.

"Well?" she demanded coolly. "Thirty seconds and counting."

Snapping out a hand, Ty caught her by the ankle, and Anny staggered, flapped her arms wildly, and sat down with a resounding thump. Lunging, Ty tried to break her fall, but he wasn't quick enough. Calling himself every name in the book, he knelt beside her and lifted her so that he could soothe the injured portion of her anatomy. Crooning broken words of apology, he held her against his shoulder while he caressed her bruised behind.

"Would you please let me go?" Anny demanded fiercely.

"Sweetheart, I didn't mean for that to happen."

"I was supposed to land on my head?"

"I couldn't just let you walk away. Did it hurt bad?"

"Of course it hurt bad!" With his hand straying in ever more intimate circles, Anny fought to maintain her anger. The last thing she needed now was to start something that would end in another fiasco.

Ty rocked her gently. "Cry, then, darling—cry so I'll know you're not really hurt." The words were whispered in her ear, but before Anny could react, she felt his large frame shaking.

He was laughing! "You think it's *funny*?" She tried her level best to sound outraged, but somehow her voice came out all soft and muddled.

"See? I'm beginning to reason the way you do," Ty chuckled. "Be a shame to let that talent go to waste, wouldn't it?"

Twisting her head to avoid his marauding lips, Anny tried again. "Ty, this has gone far enough."

"Don't be ridiculous, honey. It's barely even started yet." His eyes gleamed with laughter...and something more, something she didn't dare let herself believe in. Capturing her face between his large hands, he whispered, "This time is for you, love."

"Oh, no," Anny wailed, but Ty only laughed. He lowered her onto the quilts, following her down, and then his lips settled softly over hers and began to move.

The kiss was both a challenge and a promise. With the sweet taste of him on her tongue, the rich masculine scent of him in her nostrils, Anny didn't stand a chance. Infinitely worse, she didn't *want* to stand a chance. Not when he was holding her as though she were fragile and precious, kissing her as though he could never get enough of her.

Twisting away, she gasped for breath. "Ty, I don't think I'm very good at this sort of thing."

"We'll practice."

"Oh, Ty—"

"Okay, I won't give out reviews if you won't." His hands stroked the taut swell of her breasts, his thumbs toying with the incredibly sensitive peaks. Lowering his head, he kissed first one dusky pebble, then the other. "Sweetheart, I don't know how much you know about the effect certain medications can have on a man's... uh...prowess."

"Prowess?" Anny repeated, boldness increased by the obvious effect she was having on him. She trailed a hand down his body. "You mean...?"

The sound of his indrawn breath was like torn silk. "Like a runaway locomotive," he muttered, desperately trying to control the situation.

"No wonder you're so exhausted," Anny said, acutely disappointed to learn that she was only indirectly responsible for his ardor.

"Hey, wait a minute, I think you misunderstood me. Maybe I'd better explain a little better," Ty began, but Anny shut off his words with another kiss. There was a time and place for words, but this was neither.

With a sensitivity beyond her wildest imagination, Ty proceeded to lift her higher and higher, each time drawing back just short of the summit until she was a trembling mass of sheer craving. With lingering kisses, he explored her body, driving her to the edge of madness and then deliberately drifting off to tantalize erogenous zones she'd never even known existed.

When his tongue found the incredibly sensitive spot at the back of her knee, she cried out, "Ty, please, I can't take this anymore!"

"Then tell me what you want," he whispered, pitch-black eyes blazing into hers.

"I want *you*!" she wailed.

"How do you want me?" Sensing an auspicious bargaining position, he forced himself to hold back until he'd consolidated his gains.

"*Any* way, *all* the ways! Now!"

This time he took her slowly, building stroke by stroke, thrust by thrust, carrying her with him every step of the way until he could contain himself no longer. "Anny, Anny!" he cried out, and she was with him.

Wild the ride, higher than the moon they soared together, clinging, crying out, the salt of passion mingling with the tears of ecstasy.

Later, much later, Ty spoke again, zeroing in on the incomplete promise. "But for how long?"

"For as long as you'll stay...for always." Anny had no trouble picking up the broken threads and weaving them together again. Willingly, she handed herself—heart, soul, and body—into his keeping. She could do no less.

Ty's face contorted in an effort to hide the powerful emotion that shook him. His vision blurred as he struggled for words to express what he was feeling. "God, Anny, do you know—do you have any conception of how much you mean to me? How afraid I was?"

Her voice barely audible, Anny whispered, "Afraid?"

"I've got so little to offer you. You've got a home and a career all mapped out, and I've got nothing but a handful of ideas and enough money to see them through, but Anny, I—"

"Are you sure, Ty? This—what just happened between us, I mean—I don't want to tie you down. Some men just aren't meant to be domesticated."

"This one is. This one knows when he's home safe. And if you'll have me, beloved, then wherever we are, aboard our own fishing boat with a portable studio, in our cottage on the Inland Waterway—"

"In the pale green crystal shallows of some tropical beach," Anny put in helpfully.

"Or here at our country place after the carpenters have overhauled it from stem to stern, if you're there, I'm home."

WHAT LIES BEYOND PARADISE?

atching the pulse of a
oman in the Twenties.
A woman with a dream.
man with all his dreams
attered. The search for a
ng-lost father. And the
scovery of love.
Available from 14th
arch 1986. Price £2.50.

V●RLDWIDE

Silhouette Desire

COMING NEXT MONTH

LEADER OF THE PACK
Diana Stuart

Weylin Matthews made Jenna's dogs bark as though a wolf had walked into the camp. He seemed to have some mysterious power over her... When she looked into his eyes, she could refuse him nothing.

FALSE IMPRESSIONS
Ariel Berk

Brandon Fox didn't look like a typical girlie-joint customer — he was the handsomest man Audrey had ever seen — but he was there. And ogling was the word that certainly sprang to mind, since he couldn't seem to take his eyes off her. But first impressions are often false...

WINTER MEETING
Doreen Owens Malek

Leda knew Reardon was the one man she should avoid at all costs. But one glimpse of the pain and determination in his bleak gray eyes told her he was also the one man she could never turn away from.

COMING NEXT MONTH

GOLDEN GODDESS
Stephanie James

What right did Jarrett have to demand her love? He was the wrong kind of man, with his fanatical interest in primitive art and antiquated ideas about women. But could Hannah be wrong, and Jarrett be Mr Right . . .?

RIVER OF DREAMS
Naomi Horton

Even as Leigh reveled in his arms she knew she couldn't afford the commitment he demanded. Soon she'd have to choose . . . before the perilous cruise had run its course.

TO HAVE IT ALL
Robin Elliot

Brant's reputation preceded him, and Jenna had her doubts about getting involved. He said he wanted them to have it all, but Jenna had more in mind than Oreo cookies and a pet Canary.

Silhouette Desire

FEBRUARY TITLES

BEYOND LOVE
Ann Major

THE TENDER STRANGER
Diane Palmer

MOON MADNESS
Freda Vasilos

STARLIGHT
Penelope Wisdom

YEAR OF THE POET
Ann Hurley

A BIRD IN THE HAND
Dixie Browning

Silhouette Desire Romances

TAKE 4 THRILLING SILHOUETTE DESIRE ROMANCES
ABSOLUTELY FREE

Experience all the excitement, passion and pure joy of love. Discover fascinating stories brought to you by Silhouette's top selling authors. At last an opportunity for you to become a regular reader of Silhouette Desire. You can enjoy 6 superb new titles every month from Silhouette Reader Service, with a whole range of special benefits, a free monthly Newsletter packed with recipes, competitions and exclusive book offers. Plus information on the top Silhouette authors, a monthly guide to the stars and extra bargain offers.

**An Introductory FREE GIFT for YOU.
Turn over the page for details.**

As a special introduction we will send you FOUR specially selected Silhouette Desire romances — yours to keep FREE — when you complete and return this coupon to us.

At the same time, because we believe that you will be so thrilled with these novels, we will reserve a subscription to Silhouette Reader Service for you. Every month you will receive 6 of the very latest novels by leading romantic fiction authors, delivered direct to your door.

Postage and packing is always completely free. There is no obligation or commitment — you can cancel your subscription at any time.

It's so easy. Send no money now. Simply fill in and post the coupon today to:-

SILHOUETTE READER SERVICE, FREEPOST, P.O. Box 236 Croydon, SURREY CR9 9EL

Please note: READERS IN SOUTH AFRICA to write to:- Silhouette, Postbag X3010 Randburg 2125 S. Africa

- -

FREE BOOKS CERTIFICATE

To: Silhouette Reader Service, FREEPOST, PO Box 236, Croydon, Surrey CR9 9EL

Please send me, Free and without obligation, four specially selected Silhouette Desire Romances and reserve a Reader Service Subscription for me. If I decide to subscribe, I shall, from the beginning of the month following my free parcel of books, receive six books each month for £5.94, post and packing free. If I decide not to subscribe I shall write to you within 10 days. The free books are mine to keep in any case. I understand that I may cancel my subscription at any time simply by writing to you. I am over 18 years of age. Please write in BLOCK CAPITALS.

Name _____

Address _____

_____

_____ Postcode _____

SEND NO MONEY — TAKE NO RISKS

Remember postcodes speed delivery. Offer applies in U.K. only and is not valid to present subscribers. Silhouette reserve the right to exercise discretion in granting membership. If price changes are necessary you will be notified.
Offer limited to one per household. Offer expires April 30th, 1986.

EP18SD